THE PEACEFUL VALLEY
CRIME WAVE

The
PEACEFUL VALLEY
CRIME WAVE

Bill Pronzini

A TOM DOHERTY ASSOCIATES BOOK • NEW YORK

THE PEACEFUL VALLEY CRIME WAVE

Copyright © 2019 by Pronzini-Muller Family Trust

Design by Mary A. Wirth

Title page image: © iStockphoto / dasuan

A Forge Book
Published by Tom Doherty Associates
120 Broadway
New York, NY 10271

www.tor-forge.com

Forge® is a registered trademark of Macmillan Publishing Group, LLC.

The Library of Congress Cataloging-in-Publication Data is available upon request.

ISBN 978-0-7653-9441-5 (hardcover)
ISBN 978-0-7653-9442-2 (ebook)

Our books may be purchased in bulk for promotional, educational, or business use. Please contact your local bookseller or the Macmillan Corporate and Premium Sales Department at 1-800-221-7945, extension 5442, or by email at MacmillanSpecialMarkets@macmillan.com.

First Edition: August 2019

Printed in the United States of America

0 9 8 7 6 5 4 3 2 1

For Marcia

THE PEACEFUL VALLEY
CRIME WAVE

ONE

Peaceful Bend is a peaceful town, Peaceful Valley a peaceful place.

Now I know a lot of folks say that about where they hang their hats, some with more justification than others. It's a matter of civic pride fashioned of a sense of security and neighborly goodwill. That's the way it is in Peaceful Bend, the largest town and county seat, and all through the valley. Ranchers, farmers, merchants, businessmen all living peaceably together in as pretty a section of northwestern Montana as you could ask for, the town tucked into a crook in a fork of the Flathead River, the valley surrounded wide on three sides by timbered mountains.

It wasn't always peaceful here, of course. Way back before the century turned, when I first pinned on a badge as a young green deputy, we had our share of trouble the same as any other small settlement—renegade Indians, outlaws, rustlers, the general run of riffraff that follow the railroads, lumberjacks on a spree, and the usual land and water rights feuds between cattlemen and farmers. Took a sharp eye, a strong will, an iron fist, and now and then both ends of a Colt six-gun to tame things down. The natural flow of progress— changing attitudes, modern inventions, new laws—rounded off the rest of the rough edges.

By the time I was elected to my first term as sheriff in 1896, both the town and the county were living up to their names right proper. I don't mind saying I've had a fair hand in making and keeping it that way, the voters having kept me in office for two decades now. You won't find many citizens who'll take the name of Lucas Monk in vain. Not bragging on myself, just stating a fact.

The state has changed considerable in those two decades. More and more crisscrossing rail lines connecting it with the rest of the country. A large population growth, some fifteen million immigrants since 1900 come to work on the railroads and in the mines, smelters, and lumber camps. A homestead boom thanks to legislative acts that opened up sections in national forests and Indian tribal lands. More and more motorcars mixing in with the horse-drawn conveyances, the countryside and city streets filling up with telephone poles and hydroelectric power lines. Even flying machine exhibitions at the Fort Missoula baseball park.

Reform movements aplenty, too. Labor unions, one of 'em

the radical bunch known as the Wobblies that caused so much trouble in Butte the governor had to call in machine gun–toting National Guard troops to curb the violence, another the Nonpartisan League made up of farmers that didn't like big business and didn't support either of the political parties. Women were on the cusp of being given the vote, and about time, too—the main reason being a Missoula suffragist named Jeannette Rankin, who held rallies and meetings all over the state, including one in Peaceful Bend that drew more folks than any other event ever had, and raised enough support to convince the politicians in Helena to allow her to address the legislature. There was even talk of running her for a congressional seat on the Republican ticket come the 1916 election, which if they did and she won, would make her the first woman ever elected to Congress.

These changes affected Peaceful Bend, naturally, but not as much as they did the larger towns. Northwestern Montana is less populated than the rest of the state, our entire county having only about 1,700 souls according to the most recent census, and while Peaceful Valley isn't what you'd call isolated—Missoula, Kalispell, Helena are only a few hours away by train—we're still a small rural county with most of the land in long-held hands. Folks hereabouts tend to cling to some of the old ways of thinking and doing things.

The revolution down in Mexico and the war that had flared up in Europe a few months back had tongues wagging, but those hostilities were too far off and the particulars too mystifying for most citizens to dwell on. Seemed like

America would stay well shut of the one overseas, a good thing for the country in general and Peaceful Valley for certain. We had enough concerns of our own to occupy our thinking.

What I've been leading up to is this: There's been hardly any crime in my bailiwick the past dozen years or so. The last lethal shooting in Elk County was way back in '07, when a wheat farmer named Lamont made the mistake of ventilating a neighbor he claimed made improper advances to his wife. The worst offenses my deputies—Carse Wheeler, Boone Hudson, Ed Flanders—and I have had to deal with since are a few minor steer and sheep rustlings, chicken thievery, kids' vandalism, and an occasional drunken brawl Peaceful Bend's town marshal, Sam Prine, couldn't handle by himself. If I have to act in my official capacity more than a couple days a month, it's unusual enough to invite comment.

Anyhow, that was the way it was until mid-October, 1914.

Then, all of a sudden, I had a weeklong crime wave to deal with.

No rhyme or reason to any of what happened, no advance warning signs and only two of the offenses connected. It was as though a temporary blight had descended on Peaceful Valley, and that's no exaggeration. Crimes large and small, new mixed with old, from near comical to downright ugly that flustered and frustrated me, had me doubting myself more than once, and nearly cost me my life.

But I'm getting ahead of myself. Best I tell it as it happened, beginning with the Indian trouble. Not the kind you might think—Indian trouble like none other in the history of our sovereign state.

THE CLIMATE IN Peaceful Valley is fairly mild, considering how far north we are—the mountain ranges tend to protect us from the worst of the howling winds—but winter comes early and stays long. Fall is pretty much done with by mid-October, the red and gold and tawny seasonal colors fading, the aspens and willows and sycamores already starting to drop their leaves. The first heavy frost, which we'd had two days ago, turns the mornings sharp cold and generally means we'll be seeing snow before long. Thin skins of ice form in shadowy places even when the sun's out, so you have to watch careful where you step. I never minded winter when I was younger, but now that I'm on the cusp of the half-century mark, the cold gets into my bones and such chores as shoveling snow aren't near as easy as they once were.

I'd just come into the sheriff's office on this Friday morning and was about to start a fire in the woodstove when Henry Bandelier burst in. The courthouse has an oil furnace in the basement, but my office and the jail are at the back end and the furnace doesn't put out enough heat to suit me once the temperature starts dropping. So I'd convinced the county commissioners to have the old Vogelzang potbelly installed to warm me and my deputies, and such prisoners as we might have in the lockup, through the winter months.

Bandelier, who owns the tobacco shop on Main Street, is

the excitable sort, and this morning he was in a real dither. So flappable, in fact, with his feet dancing and his arms sawing up and down, he put me in mind of a pint-sized, red-faced albino magpie about to take flight.

"Sheriff, I been robbed!"

That brought me to attention. I didn't much care for Bandelier—he was a loudmouthed, opinionated little booger, and no more honest than he had to be—and the feeling was mutual. He'd backed my opponent in the last two elections and made critical remarks in public about me and my methods. But you don't have to care for a man to do your duty by him.

"The hell you say. When did it happen?"

"Middle of the night," he said.

"How much is missing?"

"How much? *All* of it, of course!"

"All the money in your cashbox?"

"Money? Who said anything about money?"

"Well, you did . . . didn't you?"

"No! Wasn't money that was stolen. It was my Indian."

"Come again?"

"You heard me, Sheriff. My prize wooden Indian's been pilfered."

"Now who in tarnation would steal that monstros—" I stopped, hawked my throat clear, and started over. "That Indian's been setting in front of your store six or seven years now. Weighs a hundred and fifty pounds if it weighs an ounce. Who'd want to steal it?"

"Tom Black Wolf, that's who."

"Oh, now . . ."

"It's a plain damn fact," Bandelier said. "Him and that friend of his, Charlie Walks Far. The two of 'em stole my Indian in the dead of night, and there's no getting around it."

"How do you know it was them?"

"Lloyd Cooper told me so, that's how I know. He was awake at three a.m., got out of bed to use his chamber pot. He heard a wagon rattling fast by the hotel and looked out, and Black Wolf was driving with Walks Far sitting beside him."

"How could Lloyd tell at a distance?"

"There was a moon last night," Bandelier said. "You know that as well as I do. A fat harvest moon. Lloyd saw them plain."

"Saw the wooden Indian, too?"

"Saw something eight feet long in the wagon bed, under canvas. Said it had the shape of a body. Ain't anything eight feet long that looks like a covered-up corpse, by God, except my Indian."

That was open to debate, but trying to talk sensible to a fractious individual like Henry Bandelier was akin to trying to convince a mean-spirited bull in rutting season not to be in such an all-fired hurry. I said, "Either Tom or Charlie have cause to be riled at you?"

"No. I haven't set eyes on either of 'em in two weeks or more."

"Trouble the last time you did?"

Bandelier snap-wagged his head. "They must've done it out of pure devilment."

"Devilment? They're not that kind, especially not Tom Black Wolf."

"You can't keep on sticking up for that young buck. Not after this, you can't."

"All right, just hold your water. I'll drive out to the reservation and have a talk with Tom."

"Talk with him, hell. You arrest him, you hear me? Arrest him and bring back my Indian, or else—"

"Or else what?"

He sputtered some, said lamely, "Just do your duty, Sheriff!" and turned on his heel and stalked out.

I stood for a time nibbling on a droop of my mustache and puzzling before I left the office. In my opinion the front of Bandelier's store would look a whole lot better without that wooden Indian rearing up next to the entrance, and most folks in Peaceful Bend would agree. There'd been more than one complaint about the danged thing, all of which Bandelier ignored. He was right paternal about it, which was ironical because he didn't like real Indians at all. He'd trade with the ones on the reservation, but he made them come around to the rear of his shop so as not to "offend" his white customers.

He claimed the wooden Indian had been a gift from the Cuba Libre Cigar Company of Cleveland, Ohio, in honor of the fact that he sold more Cuba Libre crooks and panatelas than any other merchant in the state, a suspect claim if ever there was one. More likely, he'd made some kind of deal with the Cuba Libre people to display the Indian, which had their name written across the chest in bold red letters, in exchange for a discount. Either way, it was an eyesore. And not just on account of its size. It had been rough-carved of some tobacco-spit brown wood, the limbs and head were some out of proportion to the body, a piece of the nose had been shot off by a drunken cowhand one Fourth of July, and the handful of cigars it was clutching were so big and phallic-looking they'd caused more than one woman to blush and look away when Bandelier first unveiled it.

Officially now, though, that wooden Indian might've been the Mona Lisa. For it was stolen property, its theft a felony offense. The law's the law, and I'm sworn to uphold it. But it sure would pain me to have to arrest Tom Black Wolf and Charlie Walks Far for the crime, if in fact they were guilty.

And if they were, what was their reason for it? That was the question uppermost in my mind, even if it wasn't uppermost in Henry Bandelier's.

What would a couple of decent live Indians want with an eight-foot, hundred and fifty pound, butt-ugly wooden Indian?

TWO

T HE MODEL T wouldn't start without I spent ten min- utes at the crank, aggravating my bursitis with every turn. Contraption never failed to give me and Carse trouble as soon as the weather turned frosty. The drive bands tended to fall out of adjustment, which caused the dang thing to creep forward so that you had to dodge out of the way while you were cranking to keep from getting run over. Clutch was prone to slipping, too.

Come the winter snows, the machine was even more of a chore. When the temperature dropped enough degrees be- low zero, like as not you'd need two men to get the motor going—one to put a blowtorch to the manifold after first blocking up the rear wheel and then to crank until his arm pretty near fell off, the other to sit inside and jiggle the spark and gas levers to keep the engine running once it got started. Then chains had to be put on the tires before you could drive out. And you had to bundle up in a lap robe as well as winter clothing to keep from freezing to death.

Progress is all well and good, and with 1915 just around the corner a county sheriff's got to have a modern conveyance or folks don't think he's serious about his job, but if you ask me, a good horse is a better asset to a man than any motorcar ever manufactured. Horses don't freeze up in the winter, and you don't have to chain their hooves so they don't slip and slide and hurl you into a snowbank or down into a ditch.

I pedaled the flivver into low gear and drove on down Main Street, the exhaust farting smoke and sparks all the way, and on out the northeast road. I paid close attention to my driving, as you'd better do if you wanted to get somewhere in one piece, but I did some ruminating, too, mostly about Tom Black Wolf.

He was twenty-two, smart as a whip, and from all indications down deep honest. Seemed to me you could trust him with your money and likely your life, which is a hell of a lot more than I'd say for a good number of white men in Peaceful Valley, Henry Bandelier being one of them. Tom had whizzed through agency school, and at the urging of Abe Fetters, the Indian agent, and Doc Olsen and me and a couple of others, he'd come in to attend high school in Peaceful Bend. Graduated at the top of his class, too.

He wanted to be an agronomist. I had to ask what that meant, first time I heard it. It means somebody who specializes in field-crop production and soil management, which is to say somebody who can make crops grow on poor land. He'd applied to a university up in Canada and been accepted and would have enrolled last semester—he'd been working jobs on and off the reservation to save up enough for his tuition—but for his grandfather, old Chief Victor, who was descended from great warrior chiefs and had been one himself during the middle of the last century. Tom just wouldn't leave the reservation while the old man was on his deathbed. Well, Chief Victor had been on his deathbed three months now and might be there another three before he finally let go. Those old warriors die reluctant.

So that was Tom Black Wolf. And Charlie Walks Far was all right, too. Not as bright as Tom, but a hard worker and no trouble to anybody. It just didn't make sense that those two, of all the people in the county, red or white or otherwise, would have swiped Bandelier's cigar company Indian. Not even as a prank. They were too law-abiding and sober-sided for that sort of foolishness.

It was fourteen miles out to the reservation, along a road that had been built for horses and wagons, not Model T Fords and their like. The flivver was contrary at the best of times; on such a road as this it kept bucking and lurching, as if it didn't much like company or my hands on its steering wheel. By the time I drove onto reservation land, my backside was sorer than if I'd been sitting a saddle for the same length of time and distance.

The reservation was mostly poor land, rocky and hilly, with not much decent bottomland. Little wonder Tom Black Wolf wanted to be an agronomist; you'd have to have special knowledge, and maybe divine help, to grow worthwhile crops in soil like this. That was the federal government for you: force Indians to live on such land and then expect them to bow down and lick your boots in gratitude. It was a hell of a thing to be born with a skin color different than the men who run the country, particularly when the country had belonged to you in the first place.

Close to three hundred Indians lived here. Mostly Salish, or Flatheads as they were called on account of the false notion started by white men that they had a tribal ritual of flattening their babies' heads, and a smattering of Kootenais, Pend d'Orielles, Piegans, mixed bloods, and breeds. Their homes were mostly slab-built shacks put up by the government back in the eighties, scattered around a small, shallow, silt-brown lagoon. There were some ramshackle barns and livestock pens—the Indians ran sheep, goats, and a few head of cattle—and an agency store and an infirmary where the poorly trained reservation doctor treated ills and disease with such medicines as the Bureau of Indian Affairs doled out. Tweaked my conscience every time I came out here, even though I'd had nothing to do with building the place or running it. It was squalor, plain and simple, two generations' worth, and no man worth his salt faces squalor with a clear conscience.

A dirt road rimmed the lagoon, and the flivver made so much noise rattling along it that kids and dogs ran and hid. Adult Indians didn't much care for the machines, either. Called them "skunk wagons" on account of the smelly exhaust fumes.

When I came up to Chief Victor's house—a cabin built larger than most on the reservation, as befitted his station— Tom Black Wolf appeared in the doorway. He was a well set up youngster, his features regular and of a color halfway between copper and bronze, his black hair shorter than most Salish wore theirs. He watched me set the brake, climb out, and walk over to him. Usually he had a smile for me, but today he was pure Indian; there wasn't any more expression on his face or in his eyes than there was on Bandelier's wooden Indian.

I didn't smile, either. I said, "Morning, Tom. Taste of snow in the air, wouldn't you say?"

"Yes, but there won't be any for another week."

"I'm glad to hear it." You want to know what the weather's going to be like, ask an Indian. They have a downright uncanny knack for predictions that more often than not turn out to be accurate.

"Have you come to see me, Sheriff Monk?"

"Some questions I need to ask. I don't want to disturb your grandfather, though. We can talk out here."

"Chief Victor has been moved to the infirmary. The doctor requested it two days ago."

"He's bad off, then?"

"It is almost his time."

"I'm sorry, Tom."

"You shouldn't be," he said. "It is only a passage. Chief

Victor has led a long and honorable life, and he will find his reward." I nodded, and Tom said then, formal, "Please come inside where it's warm."

We went in. Tom kept the place clean, and mostly neat except for books. He was quite a reader, Tom was—read anything and everything, on just about any subject you could name. Hungry for knowledge, that was Tom Black Wolf. There were books on the wood block tables and chairs and scattered in piles over the puncheon floor. Some belonged to him, bought through mail order; others were the property of the Peaceful Bend school system and Miss Mary Ellen Belknap, the school librarian and local historian. She liked Tom and allowed him to borrow as many as he wanted, despite the hidebound citizens who frowned on such generosity.

I went over and stood by the stove to thaw myself out. Tom let me warm some before he said, "Questions, Sheriff Monk?"

"On a law matter. Seems the wooden Indian that sets out in front of Henry Bandelier's tobacco shop was stolen last night. He's got a witness says you and Charlie Walks Far did the pilfering."

Tom didn't say anything.

"Did you, son? You and Charlie?"

He just looked at me with his lips pressed together. That closed-off expression gave me another twinge, for it told me he was guilty, all right, and that he wasn't going to own up to it. An Indian who respects you—and I knew Tom respected me—won't lie to your face, the way a white man will. Instead he keeps his mouth shut and lets you think whatever you like.

"Tom," I said, "stealing's a serious crime, you know that. Even if it is of a public nuisance. If you've got that wooden Indian around here somewhere, I'll find it. Go easier on you and Charlie if you tell me where it is and your reason for making off with it."

"You're welcome to search, Sheriff Monk."

"Is that all you have to say?"

He nodded. Once.

"All right, then," I said. "I'll just go ahead and see what's what around here."

There was no sign of the wooden Indian inside the shack, nor outside neither. Tom's wagon was parked out back, and I poked around some in the bed without turning up anything in the way of evidence. Finding that eight-foot chunk of wood wasn't going to be easy.

When I was done looking, Tom walked with me to the flivver. I cranked her up—motor caught right away now that it was warmed up from the drive out from town—but I wasn't ready to climb in just yet.

I said, "Been doing some saw work this morning, have you?"

The question didn't faze him. Takes a better white man than me to surprise an Indian. He said, bland as you please, "Saw work?"

"Got some specks of sawdust on your shoes. Noticed it while I was warming up at the stove."

He didn't say anything.

"Doesn't look like cottonwood or jack pine or any other tree grows on or off the reservation. Matter of fact, it looks like that tobacco-spit brown wood Henry Bandelier's statue is carved out of."

Still nothing.

"Cutting it up for winter firewood, were you?"

Silence.

"Or maybe it offended you boys somehow. That it?"

Silence.

I sighed, though not so he could hear me do it. "Reckon I'll be back, Tom," I said, and got into the flivver then and left him standing there.

I found Charlie Walks Far tending sheep on the hard-scrabble land north of the lagoon. I had to leave the Ford on the road; if I'd tried to drive up to where Charlie was, I'd have busted an axle or bruised my liver or both. But I was just wasting my time. Charlie was as closemouthed as Tom. No lies, no admissions, just civility and nothing more.

So then I went to see Abe Fetters, the Indian agent who also runs the reservation store. He didn't know anything about the wooden Indian—not that I expected him to—and was as surprised as I'd been that Tom Black Wolf and Charlie Walks Far would resort to common thievery.

"Particularly now," Abe said, "with Chief Victor so close to dying. Why, it'd be an act of disrespect, and you know how Tom idolizes his grandfather."

"I do, but it sure seems like they did it."

"They must've had a good reason, if so. But what?"

"Well, I don't know," I said. "Some ceremonial reason, maybe?"

Abe laughed without humor. "Take my word for it," he said, "there's no Salish ceremony involving a wooden Indian."

Wasn't any purpose in asking him to help me comb the village and see could we find any sign of it. Just be another waste of time. Whatever Tom and Charlie had done with it, it or what was left of it, wasn't hidden hereabouts. You'd think, big and heavy as that bugger was, they couldn't have taken it far by wagon, and you'd be right enough up to a point. But Indians are plenty resourceful when they set their minds to it. The statue could also be carried a fair distance on a travois hauled by horses or mules over one of several old trails. There's miles of reservation land, some of it rough country—the hilly sections studded with ragged outcrops and stands of lodgepole and jack pine, cut up with coulees and such. It'd take a dozen men two weeks or better to comb all of it, and even then they'd be bound to overlook any number of possible hidey-holes.

I did go to the infirmary with Abe, for I thought it proper to pay my respects, likely my last respects, to Chief Victor. But the old man was asleep, and the half-breed doctor, Joshua Teel, wouldn't let me in to see him. Chief Victor likely wouldn't recognize me anyway, Teel said. The old warrior was mostly delirious now and had been for a couple of days.

So it was a morning of frustrations all around.

Wasn't anything for me to do then but drive on back to Peaceful Bend. It was well past noon by that time, and I was almost as hungry as I was baffled. If anything, the theft made even less sense now than it had before I'd visited the reservation. Not only did it seem like a motiveless crime, but now there was the added puzzlement of why in tarnation the two young Indians would take a saw to that worthless monstrosity once they had it.

THREE

BACK IN TOWN I put the Model T away in the court-house garage and went into the sheriff's office. Carse was there, pretending to be busy looking through a stack of wanted posters; he'd heard me coming, else he'd have been sitting tilted back in his desk chair reading the latest issue of *Adventure* to while away the time. He's not exactly lazy, but he doesn't go out of his way to stir himself, neither. Tall and so beanpole thin, Carse, he looks as though a good strong wind or an open-hand slap might knock him over. But that appearance is deceptive. More than one lawbreaker has found out to their sorrow that there's plenty of grit and gristle in his bony frame. He can be plenty tough when he needs to be.

"Didn't arrest Tom Black Wolf and Charlie Walks Far, I see," he said.

"No cause yet. Henry Bandelier been blabbing about that wooden Indian of his?"

"All over town to anybody who'll listen. I take it you didn't find any sign of it on the reservation?"

I told him about the sawdust on Tom's shoes. "But that's all so far, except for what Lloyd Cooper saw and it's not enough."

"Be a shame if those boys did saw it up for firewood."

He was being ironical; he didn't like the eyesore any more than I did. I said, "Doesn't matter what they did with the dang thing. They'll still have to pay for stealing it."

"Hard to believe they'd do something like that."

"My thinking exactly."

"So what're you planning to do?"

"Have a talk with Lloyd Cooper, find out just how much he saw or didn't see last night. After that . . . I don't know yet."

"Two people been looking for you," Carse said. "Lester Smithfield, for one."

"Uh-huh. Wants to interview me about the robbery, I suppose." Lester was editor and publisher of the *Peaceful Valley Sentinel*.

"Yep. Henry Bandelier already talked to him."

"I'll just bet he did. Who else?"

"Reba Purvis telephoned. Sounded all het up. Said for you to come to her house soon as you got back."

"Het up about what?"

"Wouldn't tell me. Just said it was urgent. Said it three times."

"Uh-huh."

He grinned. "You know how she can be, Lucas."

I knew how the widow Purvis could be, all right. Nosy, bossy, full of gossip, and as if that wasn't bad enough, more than a little determined to make me her third husband. She'd outlived the other two, both of whom had surely been hastened on to their rewards by her sharp tongue and meddling ways. She was a handsome woman with some good qualities— she was president of the Ladies Aid Society and had been responsible for bringing Jeannette Rankin to Peaceful Bend to speak on woman's suffrage—and I'd had my share of lonely nights since my wife, Tess, God rest her soul, passed on four years ago. But I had no intention of being hauled off to the altar again, and then harassed into an early grave. Some other poor fellow could and probably would end up as Reba's third victim, just not me.

Had an "urgent" need to see me, did she? Either more of her female wiles or more of her gossip. The last time I'd seen her, two days ago, she'd hammered my ears with a spicy tale of young Charity Axthelm running off with an itinerant knife-carver and peddler named Rainey. How she came by all this back-fence stuff was a marvel and a mystery, the more so on account of she always seemed to ferret it out before anyone else. About half of it turned out to be false or exaggerated, but enough was credible so that when she flapped her gums, most folks paid at least some attention.

"Well, I'll go see her," I said. "But not until after I wrap myself around some grub."

"Anything you want me to do?" Carse asked.

"You eaten yet?"

"Big breakfast that'll do me until supper."

"Stay put here, then, and keep pretending to study on those wanted posters."

The land office where Lloyd Cooper works is on the way to the Elite Café, so I stopped in and had a little talk with him. Then I took my sore bones into the café for some nourishment. But before I could eat, Henry Bandelier came prancing in. He must've seen me drive past his store earlier, and that I was alone in the flivver—no Tom Black Wolf, no Charlie Walks Far, and no wooden Indian.

He sat down uninvited at my table and demanded, "Why didn't you arrest those two bucks, Sheriff?"

"On account of I got no evidence they're the guilty parties."

"No evidence? Hogwash! I told you Lloyd Cooper saw them making off with my Indian."

"That's not exactly what Lloyd saw," I said. "I talked to him myself a few minutes ago. He saw Tom and Charlie, all right, on board Tom's wagon with something in the bed under canvas, but he couldn't say for sure what it was."

"It was my Indian. You know it was!"

"I *know* no such thing. I didn't find that statue out at the reservation, nor anybody who knew anything about it." I wasn't about to mention the sawdust I'd spotted on Tom's shoes. It would only have made Bandelier madder and more cantankerous than he already was.

He shaped his lips like a man about to spit. "Just how carefully did you search?"

"Careful enough." I fixed him with a hard eye. "And I don't like your tone, Henry. You implying that I haven't done my duty?"

"If the shoe fits," he said, prissy.

"Well, it don't fit," I said. "Now suppose you take yourself back behind your store counter and let me eat my meal in peace."

"I'm warning you, Sheriff Monk . . ."

"You're doing what?"

He didn't like what he saw in my face. He scraped back his chair, not meeting my eyes now, and said to my left shoulder, "If you don't do anything about those two thieving Flatheads, then I will."

"Such as what?"

"That's my business."

"Not if it involves breaking the law. Not if you don't want me to cloud up and rain all over you."

I spoke loud, so that the five other citizens in the Elite could also hear my words plain. Bandelier's face got even redder. But he didn't sling any more words of his own; he put his back to me and walked out stiff and righteous, like a sinner leaving a tent meeting.

Well, hell, I thought. Now I'd lost my appetite.

REBA PURVIS'S TWO-STORY, scalloped and furbelowed house was on Tamarack Street, a block off the river. She lived there with her cousin, Hannah Mead, a meek little spinster whom

Reba had convinced to move up from Denver after husband number two gave up the ghost, and whom she treated more like a servant than a relative. Hannah did all the cooking and cleaning and so far as I know never complained to anybody about the chores. Hardly ever said a word in Reba's company, for that matter, struck half mute by the woman's sharp tongue and bullying.

Reba opened the door right away to my ring. "Well, it's about time, Lucas," she said in exasperated tones. "Where have you been all day?"

"Out to the reservation. Didn't Carse tell you?"

"Yes, he told me, but that wooden Indian business isn't half as important as what has happened here. Not *half*."

"What happened?"

"You won't believe such a terrible thing could happen in our community. I hardly believe it myself."

"I can't believe or disbelieve until you tell me what it is."

"Come inside."

I went in. She was het up, for a fact, her face tight-set and an angry red flush on her cheeks. There was even a worked-loose strand of her coiled sandy brown hair hanging down over her forehead. Reba was about the most fastidious woman in Peaceful Bend, always groomed neat as though she was about to attend a prayer meeting or a church social. Whatever had her in a dither must be pretty serious.

"Upstairs," she said then.

"How's that?"

"I want you to come upstairs with me."

Now I knew for sure that it was serious. Reba may have been third husband hunting, but she was too prim and proper to resort to pre-marital relations to land me or any other candidate. The few times I'd been here before, I hadn't set foot anywhere other than the front parlor and the dining room.

Up on the second floor, she said, "We must be very quiet," and when I nodded, she marched along to a closed door, eased it open about a third of the way, and stood aside so I could look in.

It was a small and frilly bedroom, her cousin's judging from the fact that the large-boned, brown-haired woman lying in the bed was Hannah Mead. She was asleep but restless, her breathing uneven, her round face pale as a grub.

When I'd had my look, Reba closed the door and led me back downstairs and into the parlor. I said, "What's this all about, Reba? Why'd you want me to look in on your cousin?"

"To see for yourself how ill she is."

"What's the matter with her?"

"She was poisoned, that's what."

That took me aback. "Poisoned?"

"That's right. Doctor Olsen doesn't believe her life is in jeopardy, though if she had drunk any more of that buttermilk than she did it would be. The poor woman might well be dead this very minute."

"Poisoned buttermilk? I never heard of such a thing."

"The poison was put into the bottle after the dairyman's delivery early this morning. It almost makes a body wish buttermilk came in cans."

Canned buttermilk. Now there was a notion. For no good

reason it put me in mind of the rhyme some cowboy wag came up with when canned milk was invented.

No teats to pull,
No hay to pitch.
Just punch a hole
In the son of a bitch.

Say that to Reba and get a smack in the eye. Hers were narrowed at me as it was. I said, "How do you mean, it was put in the bottle?"

"How do you think I mean?" she said, ominous. "The poisoning was deliberate, not accidental."

"Oh, now . . ."

"Deliberate, I tell you. Potassium cyanide. The doctor confirmed it. All that saved Hannah was the bitter almond odor."

Reba'd been right about my having trouble believing it. I nibbled on the right-side droop of my mustache, something that always set her to frowning because she didn't like the habit. Didn't like my mustache at all, any more than Tess had; according to Reba it made me look like a walrus. I'd shaved it off for Tess, grew it back when she died. A man fortunate enough to raise a fine crop ought to show it off when he's able, particularly if it helps ward off predatory females.

I said finally, "Who would do such a thing?"

"An evil person bent on cold-blooded murder."

"Murder? Why would anybody want to kill Hannah?"

Reba stepped up close. She had a way of doing that,

occupying a man's space and staring into his eyes with her big brown ones, that was discomfiting. "Not Hannah," she said. "Me."

I backed up half a step and just looked at her.

"Yes, that's right, that poisoned buttermilk was meant for me. It is only by the grace of God that I didn't drink any of it before Hannah did."

"I thought you didn't care for buttermilk—"

"I don't, but the poisoner doesn't know that."

"Reba," I said, "why would anybody want to kill *you*?"

"Why, indeed. There is only one person it could possibly be."

"Who?"

"Grace Selkirk."

It took me a few seconds to digest that. Grace Selkirk, who'd only been in Peaceful Bend a short time and worked for Titus Bedford as his housekeeper and helper in his undertaking parlor. Kept to herself and wasn't well thought of, but I'd never heard a complaint against her until now.

"What makes you think she wants you dead? You have some sort of trouble with her?"

"We had words the other day."

"Words about what?"

"Her spying on me."

"Spying?"

"I caught her skulking around out front, watching the house. Naturally I gave her a piece of my mind."

"Why would she be spying on you?"

"Titus Bedford. She has designs on him and his money."

"Oh, now. What makes you think that?"

"It's as plain as the nose on your face. Spends all her time with him, day and night, doesn't she? She may have already enticed the poor man into her bed."

"That sounds like jealousy talking, Reba. You wouldn't have your eye on Titus again, would you?"

She sniffed and stomped her foot. "Of course not! I never did have my eye on him."

Not so. Titus Bedford is a reasonably handsome and available gent in his late forties. Reba had set her sights on him for a time, and it was when he kept refusing to rise to her bait that she switched her campaign to me. Lucas Monk, second choice in the great Reba Purvis third marriage hunt. I sorely wished she'd give up on me soon, too, and pick on somebody else.

"Did you accuse her?" I asked.

"Of spying? Yes, I just told you—"

"Of having designs on Titus."

". . . Not in so many words."

Meaning she'd implied it. "What makes you so sure she was spying on you?"

"She was standing under the hawthorn tree out front, staring at the house."

"When was this?"

"Two days ago. Hannah had just come back from the mercantile, and I happened to look out through the window while I was helping her with the groceries. The Selkirk woman claimed she was just passing by and stopped a moment to rest, but I know spying when I see it." Another sniff, another foot stomp. "The woman is a witch, an evil witch."

"You didn't say that to her face?"

"No, but I should have."

Probably implied something along those lines, too. Reba and her testiness and sharp tongue. But whatever the confrontation, no matter how spirited, it was hardly provocation enough to warrant dosing a bottle of buttermilk with potassium cyanide, and I said so.

"Obviously it was sufficient provocation for the likes of Grace Selkirk," Reba said through pursed lips.

"Well, that remains to be seen."

"Not as far as I'm concerned. I want her arrested and charged before she can make another attempt on my life."

"Can't be done just because you think she has it in for you. Did Hannah overhear the words you had with her?"

"No. She was in the kitchen and there was no one else around."

"So then there's no proof—"

"Do you want to see me dead? Of course you don't. Well, then, you just go and find some and put that woman in jail."

"Me? My jurisdiction is the county, the town is Sam Prine's—"

"Pshaw! Sam Prine is nothing more than a glorified watchman, and not very bright. I want *you* to handle this matter."

"Now, Reba—"

"You, Lucas, and I won't take no for an answer. You're the

only law officer qualified to deal with a devilish matter like this. You know that as well as I do."

Well, she had a point. Sam Prine was a good man, but he had zero experience in criminal investigation. And I had to admit that Reba was right about his limited smarts; brawn was his main qualification for the town marshal's job. I could overlook the fact that Peaceful Bend wasn't my jurisdiction—Sam wouldn't mind and neither would anybody else. But I didn't like Reba ordering me to do her bidding and arrest somebody without proper evidence, the same as Henry Bandelier had, and I said so.

She sniffed again, in a hurt kind of way. "I am frightened for my life. You can see that, can't you?"

Oh, hell. She wasn't exaggerating about being scared, that was plain enough. "All right," I said, "I'll do some investigating. And talk to Grace Selkirk, but unless she confesses to malicious mischief—"

"Malicious mischief!"

"—or attempted homicide, that's all I can do. Meanwhile, you be careful of what you eat and drink."

"I certainly will. And if you don't arrest that woman and she comes skulking around my property again, she'll find herself on the receiving end of a bullet. I have already loaded Fred's old pistol and I know how to use it."

There wasn't any use warning her against going off half-cocked. Maybe later she'd be in a frame of mind to listen to sensible advice, but sure not right now. I said I'd best be tending to business.

Reba went with me to the door, where she stepped up close again and laid her hand tight on my arm. She had fingers like a clamp when she was upset. "You'll come back after you've spoken to the witch?"

"I'll be back," I said, but what I didn't say was how soon.

FOUR

THERE WASN'T ANY use in canvassing Reba's neighbors. The nearest ones on the side where she had her dairy products delivered were the Eldredge sisters, a pair of elderly spinsters who minded their own business and weren't likely to be up and peering out their windows at 5:30 a.m. Besides which, Reba's side yard was thick with caragana, rosebushes, and other plantings. Her front yard was on the jungley side, too, not that whoever had put the poison in the buttermilk bottle would have risked going onto the property from Tamarack Street. Out back was a carriageway lined with cottonwoods that'd be ink-black at that pre-dawn hour.

I took a look around the side porch area. Didn't expect to find anything, didn't find anything. Easy as pie for somebody to slip up there after the delivery was made, take off the bottle cap, put the potassium cyanide inside, close it up again, and slip away in the dark. Wouldn't have taken more than a couple of minutes.

Wasn't any use in talking to the milkman, either. The would-be poisoner would've been careful not to be seen lurking. So I went instead to the marshal's office, in a separate building behind the courthouse. Sam Prine sleeps in the back room, which is what he was doing when I got there. Just as well. I'd had it in mind to tell him about the poisoning and then swear him to keep his lip buttoned, but there really wasn't any need for him to know. It'd just fluster him. And he wouldn't welcome the confidence any more than he would the responsibility of investigating. So with my mind changed, I left without waking him up.

Doc Olsen had his office above the Merchant's Bank two blocks north. Doc was in and treating young Tyler Fix, whose brother, Grover, owned the Fix Mercantile Company, for something or other in what he calls his surgery. Doc is a funny old bird, thin as a rail with big knobby hands and what Reba calls a caustic sense of humor. I remember him saying once when asked what a particular patient had been suffering from, "The cortex of the brain was unnaturally flushed, the neuronic synapses extended enough to inhibit the nervous impulse from axon to dendrite in such a fashion as to make his muscular articulation erratic." I memorized that when he explained it meant the man was drunk.

Doc finished with Tyler and sent the kid on his way with a tube of skin ointment. While Doc washed up, I quizzed him about the poisoning.

"No doubt that it was potassium cyanide," he said. "You can't mistake that bitter almond odor. Or Hannah's symptoms—rapid breathing, dizziness, nausea, headache."

"Enough to have killed her if she'd swallowed a full glass?"

"Probably. Have to have the buttermilk analyzed to be positive."

"You have the bottle, Doc?"

"In my refrigerator."

"Good. Can you do the analysis?"

"I don't have the equipment. Have to send it down to Missoula."

"No need yet, I guess. Just hold it for evidence."

"Naturally. Unless I decide to drink some of it myself, put an end to all my sorrows and annoyances."

"Hah. Reba tell you she thinks the poison was meant for her?"

"No," Doc said, "but I gathered she did from the way she carried on. She can be difficult, we both know that, but who'd want to kill her?"

"She's got somebody in mind. She tell you who?"

"No."

"Well, she told me, but I don't want to say who until I do some investigating."

He shook his big shaggy head. "Poisoned buttermilk. Last thing I'd have expected to happen in Peaceful Bend."

"Makes two of us."

"I wouldn't have expected anybody to steal that cigar store Indian, either," he said as I started out. "You find it on the reservation?"

"Not yet."

"Henry Bandelier's pretty worked up about the theft."

"Not half as worked up as Reba is," I said, "with a whole lot more cause."

TITUS BEDFORD HAD been the only undertaker in Peaceful Bend for some while, but the town was growing, if growing slow, and Titus took to fretting that some other mortician would move in and open a fancy establishment and take away a good portion of his business. So he decided to build his own fancy establishment first, in a better location than the rented building down near the train depot—a new place big enough for embalming and viewing, and to show off and store his caskets and plain boxes.

The spot he picked was on the Cherry Street side of his property east of Main, his house facing on the next street over, Anaconda. The new building had a plate glass window in front so folks walking or riding by could look in and see the trimmed display coffins with their satin linings and feather pillows and shiny brass fittings. He also put in a brick driveway wide enough to accommodate his new Cunningham carved-panel motor hearse.

Titus bought all his rough pine boxes and fancier coffins from a casket maker in Missoula. Used to have the more extensive coffins trimmed by his wife, Maude, before she passed on and then by the widow Brantley until she died sudden of a coronary; he bought the caskets without linings on account of it was thriftier that way, and Titus is nothing if not thrifty.

He hadn't been open for business long in the new location when Grace Selkirk arrived in town. No one knew where she'd come from or why she'd picked Peaceful Bend to settle in. Just came in on the train one day and took a room at the Valley Hotel while she hunted for a job. Didn't have to hunt long, since Titus had put an ad in the *Sentinel* for a seamstress. Wasn't long before Grace Selkirk was not only working in the widow Brantley's stead at the funeral parlor, but living in one of Titus's spare rooms and keeping house for him.

Tongues started to wag right off. Gossip's a major industry in any small town, and in Peaceful Bend the women, especially Reba Purvis, and the male members of the Hot Stove League that hang out at the Commercial Club work the hardest at it. More gossip comes my way, I reckon, than just about anyone in town, most of it from Reba.

Grace Selkirk looked to be a couple of years past thirty and was not hard on the eye, in a chilly sort of way. Before long, folks had her and Titus sharing a bed. Some even went so far as to claim he'd met her on one of his casket-buying trips to Missoula and brought her back with him on the sly so they could live together in sin.

I wasn't sure I believed any of it. I've known Titus for a lot of years; there's not many more morally upright citizens in Peaceful Valley. Not that that necessarily prevented him from being interested in Grace Selkirk as more than an employee, but it'd be an eyebrow-lifter for me to find out he was. All he'd ever said about her in my hearing was that she was a good cook and housekeeper, and a better coffin trimmer than Maude or the widow Brantley. An artist with silk and satin, according to him, taking pains to get the folds in the lining and the fluff in the pillows just so. Her finished caskets were what he called funerary works of art.

Nobody liked Grace Selkirk much. She never made any effort to be neighborly and little enough to be civil. Stayed close to Titus's home and the undertaking parlor. Old Ben Downey, one of the Hot Stove League, passed a remark about her one day that I happened to overhear; it caused hoots of laughter and got told all over town for days afterward. Ben spit against the hot side of the cast-iron stove in the Commercial Club, waited for it to sizzle, and allowed as how he knew for a fact that those rumors about her and Titus were false. One of the other loafers asked him how he knew, and Ben said, "Titus is still alive, ain't he? First time he stuck his tallywhacker in that woman, him and it would of froze solid."

As I trod the brick walk to the mortuary entrance, I thought about Reba's accusation that Grace Selkirk had her sights set on marrying Titus and viewed Reba as a rival. But even if that were true and they'd had words over it, it seemed like a mighty thin motive for attempted homicide. Unless of course the Selkirk woman was as crazy as a laying hen with a half-stuck egg.

The little bell over the door tinkled discreetly when I stepped into the empty reception room. My nostrils pinched up at the lingering smell of flowers mingled with the strong pickle-like odor of formaldehyde; you weren't supposed to smell the formaldehyde in this part of the building, the embalming room being at the rear, but I've got a sharp sniffer and I always could. Didn't like the combination one bit. It made sitting through funerals, Tess's funeral in particular, even more of an ordeal.

Titus came in wearing his usual black suit and solemn expression, but his face smoothed out some when he saw me. "Good afternoon, Lucas. What brings you here?"

"I'd like a few words with Miz Selkirk, if she's available."

"She is, in the sewing room."

"Been here all day, has she?"

"Yes, since eight o'clock."

"You're an early riser, Titus. Up at the crack of dawn, as I recall. She happen to leave your house between six and seven this morning?"

"Not as far as I know, she didn't."

"Not even for, say, ten minutes or so?"

He said, "I suppose she could have left for that long, while I was, ah, occupied." His brow wrinkled up. "Why all the questions? Has something happened?"

"Something has," I said, "and you'll hear about it soon enough. Right now I'd like a word in private with Miz Selkirk. Ask her to step in."

Titus is not a man to argue with anybody, much less the law. He went out without another word. I paced around for two or three minutes, smelling flowers and formaldehyde, before Grace Selkirk came in alone.

She wore black, too, a plain dress with white lace at the throat and on the sleeve cuffs. Like every other time I'd seen her, her black hair—dyed black with shoe polish, the way it looked—was braided and tightly coiled around her head. Her ice-blue eyes and pale face showed no emotion of any kind. Cold woman, for a fact.

"You wish to speak to me, Sheriff?"

"I do. Mind telling me if you had occasion to leave Mr. Bedford's home early this morning, around the time the man from Miller's Dairy makes his deliveries?"

"I did not."

"You know where Reba Purvis lives?"

"Reba Purvis? No."

"But you know who she is."

"Yes."

"Get along with her?"

"I've only spoken to the woman once. Why do you ask?"

"Her housekeeper was poisoned this morning. Poisoned buttermilk that Mrs. Purvis thinks was intended for her."

I thought that might shake the woman some, or at least produce a twitch or two. Nothing. She stood there same as before, straight as a stick, her frosty eyes flat-fixed on mine. They hardly ever blinked, those eyes. Gave you a creepy feeling when you looked into them long enough.

"What does that have to do with me?" she said.

"Lucky thing Hannah Mead didn't drink a whole glass or she'd be dead now. Pretty sick as it is. Doesn't seem as though you much care."

"I don't know Hannah Mead."

"Person ought to have sympathy for anybody poisoned with potassium cyanide."

"Are you suggesting I put the poison in the buttermilk?"

THE PEACEFUL VALLEY CRIME WAVE

"Did you?"

"Certainly not. What possible reason would I have to want to harm Reba Purvis?"

"Maybe on account of she once set her cap for Mr. Bedford and might still want to marry him."

"Why should that matter to me?"

"It would if you have similar intentions."

She made a derisive noise, a kind of ladylike snort. "My relationship with Mr. Bedford is strictly that of employer and employee."

"You're not interested in marriage, then?"

"Not with him or any other man."

"Did you have an argument with Mrs. Purvis the other morning, out in front of her house?"

"Yes. She accused me of spying on her, a ridiculous charge. I was merely passing by and stopped for a moment to rest. I told her so and she became abusive."

"What did you do then?"

"Simply walked away."

"So you have no animosity toward her."

"Not until now. If she persists in making slanderous accusations against me, I will consult an attorney. Kindly tell her that. Now if you have no more questions, Sheriff, I have my sewing to attend to."

Well, hell's bells. It was her word against Reba's, and I'd known Reba to jump to conclusions and exaggerate to beat the band. There wasn't a shred of proof that Grace Selkirk poisoned the buttermilk, or any good reason I could see why she would have. I let her go on about her business while I went on about mine.

"I TOLD YOU she was a witch!" Reba cried. "Didn't I tell you she was? A murderous witch!"

"That may be, but—"

"She *did* poison the buttermilk. I have no other enemies, it couldn't be anyone else. Or do you choose to believe her instead of me?"

"Sure not, but—"

"If she succeeds in slaughtering me, my death will be on your head, Lucas Monk."

I swallowed a sigh. I hadn't relished coming back to her house to tell her about my talk with Grace Selkirk, but I had to do it. Naturally it threw her into a tizzy and brought the expected load of wrath down on my head. Not that I blamed her for being upset. I just didn't much care for being castigated for something beyond my control and that was no fault of mine.

"You're not in any more danger," I said. "If the Selkirk woman is guilty, she knows now that I've got my eye on her. She wouldn't dare make another attempt on your life."

"You can't be sure of that unless you watch her twenty-four hours a day. Or me twenty-four hours a day."

I let that pass. "What would you have me do, Reba? My hands are tied without evidence."

"Find the potassium cyanide she used. Search her room in Titus's house."

"I can't do that without a warrant. And I can't get a warrant without cause enough to convince Judge Peterson. Besides, she'd be smart enough to hide the poison someplace or get rid of it."

"Then for heaven's sake find out where she got it. Talk to Adam Peach at the drugstore."

"You can't buy potassium cyanide in a drugstore," I said. "Only way I know to get it is from apricot pits, almonds, cassava roots. Then chemicals have to be added to the powder."

"You see? She is a witch. Only a witch would know how to mix up such a devil's concoction."

Wasn't anything I could say to that. For one thing, just about anybody, if they set their mind to it, could learn how to make the stuff by reading a chemistry book or a book on poisons. For another thing, it wasn't likely a private citizen could extract and mix up a batch of potassium cyanide in less than twenty-four hours. Barring that witch nonsense, why would Grace Selkirk have some already made and on hand? But Reba wasn't in a frame of mind to listen to sensible explanations.

"What kind of chemicals?" she said.

"How's that?"

"You said the poison has to be mixed with chemicals. What kind?"

"I don't rightly know."

"Well, find out and ask Adam if he sold any of those to her."

"I doubt they're the kind that'd be stocked in a drugstore. Even if they were, Grace Selkirk wouldn't likely buy them in her own backyard."

Reba made a sound in her throat like a wasp caught in a spiderweb. "So you're not going to do anything at all," she said.

"You needn't fret about that. I'll do all I'm empowered to do, and one way or another I'll get to the bottom of this business. Meanwhile, I'll ask you not to say anything to anybody about what happened to Hannah with that poisoned buttermilk. And that goes double for making any more unfounded accusations against Grace Selkirk. She's liable to bring a suit against you for slander if you do; she as much as told me she'd do just that."

"Witch!"

"Reba—"

"Very well, I'll keep this foul business to myself for the time being," she said, harsh and stiff, "but you had *better* get to the bottom of it, Sheriff." Sheriff this time, not Lucas. "For your sake as well as mine."

FIVE

THE THIRD AND most shocking crime in the sudden epidemic reared its ugly head the next afternoon.

Saturdays are a busy market day in Peaceful Bend. Folks come in from the ranches and farms and outlying hamlets to do their weekly shopping, socialize with friends, get haircuts and shaves, and treat themselves to sodas and ice cream at Peach's Drugstore or beer and stronger spirits in one of the saloons before heading back home. Mornings when I'm not busy with sheriff's matters, I spruce up some in a starched white shirt, string tie, and my best suit, clap my stockman's Stetson on my head, and walk around town saying howdy to those I haven't seen in a while. My political opponents claim it's calculated to curry favor with the voters, but that's not how I look at it. I figure it's incumbent on a public official to be neighborly and make himself available to listen to comments, suggestions, and complaints from the people he serves.

Before I got around to that activity I went to see how Hannah Mead was getting on. Still in her bed but recovering, Reba told me, tight-lipped. She wouldn't take me upstairs this time. Wasn't any need for me to talk to Hannah, she said; she'd already told me everything there was to tell. Still peeved at me for not clapping Grace Selkirk in irons on her say-so. I didn't tell her that I'd had a careful roundabout conversation with Adam Peach after leaving her the day before, and as I figured, he hadn't sold anything to anybody recently that could be used to make potassium cyanide. Such news would only have started her haranguing me again.

Lester Smithfield buttonholed me on my way back to Main Street. He wanted to know how my investigation into the stolen wooden Indian was progressing, and scolded me for not coming to see him yesterday. What with the buttermilk poisoning business, I'd totally forgotten that he'd come to the sheriff's office asking for me. I apologized, and told him as much as I deemed proper for public consumption. Lester is one of my staunchest supporters, but he's also a newshound who needs to be fed regular to keep him happy.

Otherwise it was a normal Saturday morning made even more palatable by the fact that Henry Bandelier stayed clear of me. The afternoon started out normal, too. After an early lunch at the Valley Hotel, I walked over to the Municipal Park baseball diamond. Baseball is real popular in the spring and summer, with a game just about every week—school and pick-up matches, and contests between the Peaceful Bend Bobcats and teams from Elkton, the only other town of any size in the valley, and towns in the nearby counties. I reckon I'm as big an addict as anybody; attend as many local games as I can, keep tabs on the Major Leagues in the big-city newspapers that come in by train. One of my fondest wishes is to one day sit in the stands in Detroit or Washington and watch Ty Cobb bat against Walter Johnson, not that that's ever likely to happen. Farthest out of Montana I've ever gone or am ever likely to is Laramie, Wyoming, to pick up a wanted felon.

Today was crisp-cold and sunny, with that hint of winter in the air, but just as I expected, a handful of kids were out there on the field taking turns hitting and chasing fly balls. I sat down to watch them. That was where I was and what I was doing when Jeb Barrett came rattling up fast in his ranch wagon, calling my name.

"Figured I'd find you here, Sheriff," he said. He was a baseball addict himself, plays first base for the Bobcats. Good-humored gent, Jeb, but he wasn't cheerful today. Just the opposite, his lean face drawn tight and grim. "Something bad's happened. Real bad."

"What is it?"

"My two boys went poking around over at the old Crockett place this morning. Weren't supposed to trespass, but you know how kids are. They got it into their heads to pull off the cover on what's left of the dry well, and when they saw what was down inside, they come racing home to tell me. I thought they were funning me at first, but when I rode over there and had a look for myself, I come straight in to fetch you."

"What's in that well, Jeb?"

"A dead woman. Young girl, looks like."

"Sweet Jesus." After twenty years and all I've had to contend with in that time I'm not easily shocked, but the thought of a young girl dead in the well on the abandoned Crockett property was enough to turn my insides to ice. "Could you tell who she was?"

"Not for sure. She's lying twenty feet down on a pile of rubble, facedown. But she appears young and slim and she's got long blond hair. It could be Charity Axthelm."

Charity Axthelm. The ranch girl Reba'd told me had run off with the traveling peddler three days ago.

"How long you figure she's been in there?"

"Not long enough for . . . well, you know."

No smell of decay, he meant. "Any sign of violence on the body?"

"Hard to tell from a distance." He let out a heavy breath. "But she sure didn't fall into the well by accident. The cover was on it. My boys been messing around over there before, and Doyle swears the other times the cover was off and laying on the ground. Somebody had to've slid it back on."

I climbed onto the seat beside him and Jeb drove us quick to the courthouse. Boone Hudson happened to be in the sheriff's office today; he lives in Elkton, up in the northeastern part of the county, and patrols that section of the valley. Carse was there with him, the two of them playing checkers. I told them what Jeb had told me, sent Boone to inform Doc Olsen, sent Jeb on his way back to the Crockett place, and took Carse with me to the garage to crank up the Model T.

For a change the motor caught without much fuss. I let Carse drive; he's better at negotiating road ruts than I am, and less apt to blister the air with oaths when one of 'em comes near cracking a man's spine.

What was left of the Crockett farm was two miles east of town, adjacent to Jeb Barrett's property on Little Bear Creek—one of several valley farms that had been abandoned, though not for the same reason as most. The land's good, but not all the homesteaders who flocked to Montana the past decade or so were willing or able to work it hard enough and long enough to make a worthwhile living. Seth Crockett was one of those. Too lazy, and too fond of liquor to boot. His place was already run down, the unpruned trees in his plum orchard getting stunted and gnarly, when he dropped dead one afternoon while tending to his meager hay crop. He hadn't been in the ground more than a week when his long-suffering wife auctioned off most of their belongings, packed up herself and their one offspring, and went to live with her folks in South Dakota. The farm had been for sale for more than a year now with no takers. Unless somebody bought it soon, the county would take it over and sell it for back taxes.

Jeb was just turning his wagon onto the overgrown access lane when the flivver came belching and snorting up behind him. Doc Olsen's Tin Lizzie was weaving along some distance behind us, Doc at the wheel and Boone hanging on for dear life beside him. Doc drives that machine of his the way he used to drive his buggy, which is to say poorly and not a little reckless.

The weedy lane passed through barren fields, up over a rise, and down into the farmyard. The house, small barn, and lean-to stable were tumbledown, with missing boards and shingles, and the poorly built chicken coop had collapsed in on itself; altogether the buildings had a desolate look in the pale sunlight. Creepers and wild climbing roses covered one wall of the house and half the sagging porch roof. Tall summer-brown grass and weeds made a jungle of the yard and what had once been a vegetable garden. The old well, if I remembered correctly, was behind the farmhouse.

Jeb stopped his wagon and Carse rattled the flivver up behind. The oldest Barrett son, Doyle, was waiting for us along with Jeb. He's big for his age, about twelve, and usually had a kid's swagger about him. Not today. He looked relieved to see his pa and the county law, as if being alone here with the poor dead girl had spooked him some. I didn't blame him. The cold, gusty wind made noises like ghosts moaning and wailing.

We all trudged around to where the old well was, picking our way past gopher holes, rocks, scattered pieces of rotted wood, and avoiding thick tangles of wild blackberry. Seth Crockett had had the same poor sense when it came to locating his first well that he'd had in tending to his land. If it had been dug deeper and farther away from the house, it wouldn't have gone dry and made it necessary for him to have

another dug over near the creek where the first one should
have gone.

Wasn't much left of the old well, the windlass having collapsed into rubble. The warped wooden cover, two halves
held together by rusted hinges, had been put back on top by
Jeb or Doyle or both; Carse hauled it free. My stomach roiled
when I looked down inside. I could see the girl plain, lying
in a twisted sprawl on the clutter of dirt and stones that
had crumbled loose from the walls. Long strands of blond
hair spread out around her head, the tails of a sheepskin
coat bunched around her, the blue gingham dress underneath hiked partway up her bare legs. I couldn't make out
any wounds or blood. If there were any such, they were on her
front side.

Beside me Carse said, "Good God Almighty."

"Amen."

"If some son of a bitch threw her down there, I hope he
rots in hell."

Doc Olsen's Tin Lizzie rattled and snorted into the farmyard. I went back out there, Carse and the Barretts following. Doc had brought his bag and an old military blanket to
wrap the body in. Carse fetched the rope we kept in the flivver's trunk box. Wasn't any question of driving either of the
Model Ts around to where the well was; the rocks and gopher holes would sure have busted an axle or a wooden ar-
tillery wheel if we'd tried it. Jeb thought he could maneuver
his wagon all the way around, and he managed it all right,
got it drawn up fairly close to the well.

While that was being done, Doc had his look down at the dead girl. "Hasn't been in there long," he said after sniffing the air. "Good thing it's been cold lately."

"Jeb thinks she might be Charity Axthelm."

"Well, we'll find out."

Carse and Jeb fastened the ropes to the wagon, then found stones to anchor the wheels. Boone was too heavy to be the one to go down into the well, and Carse is ten years younger than me, more agile, and not afflicted with bursitis. That left the unpleasant task to him.

He tied the longest rope around his waist and climbed down with Doc's blanket. He made short work of wrapping and tying up the body, and Jeb and Boone and me hauled it up. Then we dropped the rope back down and helped pull Carse back onto solid ground.

"Charity Axthelm, all right," he said. He looked a little sick.

Doc said, "Put the body in the wagon. Then everybody back off and let me have a look at her."

While he was doing his examining, I told Carse and Boone to hunt around and see could they find anything that might tell us who was out here with the dead girl. Then I took Jeb and his son aside.

"Your pa tells me the well cover was on the ground the other times you and your brother came fooling around over here," I said to Doyle. "You sure about that?"

"Yes, sir. We looked into the well a couple of times before. When we saw the cover was on today, we wondered how come. That's why we took it off and looked in."

"How'd you and Kyle get over here today? Horseback?"

"Yes, sir. Too far to walk from our place."

"When you rode in, did you notice was there any sign of recent passage on the lane? Horse tracks? Wagon or automobile tracks?"

"Well . . . the grass was beat down some."

"Yes, it was," Jeb said. "I noticed that, too, when I drove in earlier."

"Beat down by what, would you say?"

"Hard to tell. Could've been a wagon or motorcar."

"Were the tracks cut deep enough to've been made by the wheels on a heavy, loaded wagon?"

"Didn't look that deep, no."

A chorus of honks sounded overhead. Another flock of wild geese headed south for the winter. When they were gone, I said, "Either of you see anybody in this vicinity recently who doesn't live around here? That itinerant peddler, Rainey, that was in the valley last week, for instance?"

Doyle shook his head. Jeb said, "Didn't come out this way, far as I know. Why? You suspect him, Sheriff?"

"No cause to suspect anybody until I know for sure how the girl died."

I knew for sure three minutes later, when Doc Olsen finished his preliminary examination. "Cause of death appears to be manual strangulation," he told me. "Deep bruises on her throat and neck. The broken neck most likely happened when her body was thrown into the well."

"So now we definitely got us a murder on our hands."

"You have, Lucas. I'm only a doctor and glad of it."

"And the county coroner."

He said, testy, "I don't need you to remind me of my duties."

"One of which is calling a coroner's jury. You figure on doing that right away?"

"I hadn't thought that far."

"I'd take it as a favor if you'd hold off until Monday," I said. "Give me time to do some investigating, maybe find out enough so the jury can render a more informed verdict. Any objection?"

"No, no objection. They're just a legal formality anyway."

For a fact they were. Nine men to look at the body and see for themselves how she'd died, listen to testimony from witnesses such as Jeb and Carse and me, and unless there was strong evidence as to who was responsible, make the usual determination of death at the hands of person or persons unknown.

I said, "Now then, Doc. Was the girl molested?"

"Doesn't seem to have been, underclothing all in place, but I can't be certain until I make a complete examination."

"Any other marks on the body?"

"None except some scratches and damage from insects," he said, the last being more information than I needed to know right now. "Evidently no animals or rodents got at her."

Thank the good Lord for that, at least.

Ordinarily when there's a death in the valley this close to town, I'd send for Titus Bedford and his hearse. Not in this case, though. I didn't want word about what had happened here to get out before the coroner's jury convened, so I'd have

time to investigate. It might anyway, but not for lack of trying to keep it under wraps.

I swore everyone to secrecy until Monday. Nobody ob-
jected, though Jeb grumbled a bit about having to take part
of a workday off to testify. Then Boone and Carse transferred
the body from Jeb's wagon to the backseat of Doc's Tin
Lizzie and covered it up with a piece of canvas Jeb had. Doc
said he'd drive in roundabout to the funeral parlor, avoiding
the center of town, and caution Titus Bedford to keep mum
when he got there. He and Boone left in the Tin Lizzie, Jeb
and his son in their wagon. I had Carse stay put with me.
He knew why without me saying anything.

When the others were gone, the two of us did some more
searching of the area around the well and out in the farmyard. He and Boone hadn't found anything, and he and I
didn't, either. Not until we went to take a look inside the
farmhouse.

The doors and windows had been boarded up, but the
boards across the front door had been loosened so that you
could pull them aside and walk right in. The interior was full
of dust and spiderwebs, smelled of mildew and dry rot. But
somebody had been in here not too long ago. There were
scuff and smear marks and footprints in the dust on the parlor floor. Hadn't been the Barrett kids; one clear footprint
was a man's, a fairly big man judging from its size, and another was narrow and short enough to've been made by a
woman.

A few unsold and discarded furnishings were left in the
parlor—a broken-legged table, a whitewashed cabinet with

one door missing and the other hanging askew from its hinges, and a ripped-up horsehair sofa with some of its springs showing. The sofa was what held my attention after I was done looking at the floor. It had a blanket on it, and not a tattered, dirty one. I picked up the blanket, looked it over. Plain, ordinary, the kind you can buy just about anywhere. Not new, but fairly clean.

Carse, who's about as sharp-eyed as me, said, "You thinking what I'm thinking?"

"Most likely." I poked around on the sofa. Between two of the cushions was a hairpin that was too bright to've been there long. Wasn't anything else on or in the sofa, but when I moved it so I could look underneath, I found something there.

"That a button?" Carse asked.

"Yep. Torn off a man's brown jacket, looks like. Not much doubt now the girl was meeting somebody here on the sly." Not that that was much of a surprise. According to Reba, Charity Axthelm had a reputation for being man-hungry and free and easy with her favors.

"Same man who killed her?"

"Maybe."

"The peddler, Rainey?"

"Maybe," I said again. I gestured at the marks in the dust. "Looks to me like she was strangled in here and then her body carried out and dumped into the well."

"The killer figuring that with winter coming, there'd be no chance of it being found until spring."

"And hoping it might never be."

"But why'd he kill her, a pretty young thing like that?"

"Find that out when we find him," I said. "I reckon we're done in here for now. We got more unpleasant business to attend to, and it's time we got to it and got it over with."

Carse grimaced. He didn't say anything, but I knew he was wishing he didn't have to be part of it. I didn't blame him; hell, I didn't want any part of it, either. But it had to be done, and I was in no frame of mind to face the chore alone.

SIX

THE AXTHELM RANCH was over to the east, just about three miles from the Crockett property and double the distance from town. I'd been there maybe four times, the first to offer a hospitable welcome when the family moved here from Nebraska in '06, the others when I was stumping for votes during election time. It was a fairly small spread on land good for cattle and hay that J. T. Axthelm had inherited when his uncle passed on. He'd not only kept it up, but made improvements. Ran about the same number of cows old Frank Axthelm had, fifty or sixty head; owned a few horses, a few pigs, a flock of chickens.

He wasn't an easy man to know. Civil enough when you saw him, but he didn't talk much and kept himself and his affairs more private than most. Whatever the initials stood for I never found out; he'd signed J.T. Axthelm on the tax roles and voter registration forms. We weren't on a first-name basis, anyhow. I did know that he'd ridden with Teddy Roosevelt's Rough Riders during the Spanish-American War, and that a wound he'd received on the San Juan Hill skirmish was the reason he walked with a limp; I'd got that information from his son, Bob. His wife, Miriam was her given name, was on the quiet side, too, and neither of them socialized much.

Bob and Charity, on the other hand, were both outgoing youngsters. They came into Peaceful Bend regular before and after they graduated school—he was twenty-one now and she'd been two years younger, both of them good-looking and popular. You'd see one or both at the community hall dances and picnics and other social functions. Charity had never lacked for male attention and had a flirtatious streak, but I hadn't put much stock in Reba's gossipy claim that the girl was promiscuous. Until now, after what we'd found in the Crockett farmhouse.

I was still wrangling with myself as what to say to her parents when Carse drove us through the Axthlems' gate. The house was good-sized, another room and a screened back porch having been added. House and barn and a scatter of outbuildings—corral, pigpen, brooder house, shed to keep farm implements out of the weather—were all in good repair. Same with the fenced hayfields and cattle graze. A nice piece of property, all told.

The noise the flivver made brought Mrs. Axthelm out of the house and her husband limping from the barn. Carse left the engine running and he and I stepped down. I still

hadn't decided how much to tell of what we knew and suspected. One thing I had settled on: I'd deliver the blow
straight out, and only to him. Looking at the girl's mother
was like looking at an older, careworn version of her daughter.
I figured she'd break down when she was told, and if there's
one thing I can't bear, it's watching a woman, especially a
newly bereaved woman, weep and carry on. The sight near
unmans me every time.

Axthelm nodded to Carse and said to me, "Sheriff. What
brings you out here?"

"Need to talk to you privately, Mr. Axthelm."

He didn't waste time or words. "Miriam, go back inside."

She didn't argue, just turned on her heel and disappeared
into the house. The set of her slender back and shoulders said
she knew it was bad news. Axthelm knew it, too. He stood
straight-backed, head up, gnarled hands held close against
his sides.

"Well?" he said.

"I'm afraid we've got bad news. About your daughter.
She—" The rest of it got stuck. I swallowed and coughed to
clear my voice box.

"Get it said, Sheriff."

"I'm sorry, real sorry to have to say this, but she's dead."

He took it without flinching, without moving a muscle.
Just stood there board-stiff for what seemed like a long
time. "How?" he said finally, and his voice hadn't changed,
either. He had a tight rein on his feelings, as tight as a man
can have at such a time as this.

"Killed. Found a little while ago on the Crockett property."

"Where?"

"The abandoned farm a few miles from here."

"Killed how?"

I got the rest of it out quick. "Looks like somebody choked her to death, then put her body down an old dry well. Two, three days ago. Jeb Barrett's boys were fooling around over there this morning and they found her."

"Somebody," Axthelm said. "Who?"

"Don't know yet. Could be that fella Rainey, but—"

"Who's Rainey?"

"The traveling peddler that was in the area the past three weeks or so. Your daughter never mentioned him?"

"No. Why should she?"

"Word was she took a shine to him."

"Meaning what?"

"Well . . . sorry again, but enough of a shine to run off with him."

A muscle jumped on Axthelm's jaw. "Who told you that?"

"Local gossip."

"Bullshit. Charity wasn't that kind."

I had a short nibble on my mustache, hawked my throat clear again. "She'd been in that well two or three days, like I said. Where'd you think she was all that time?"

"Kalispell, with her brother. Bob went up there on ranch business. She was supposed to go with him."

"You didn't hear from Bob to say she didn't?"

"No. Must've figured she changed her mind."

Axthelm spoke in the same flat monotone, but I sensed that he wasn't giving me the straight truth. That maybe he knew about her planning to run off with Rainey, or suspicioned it, and was lying to protect her name. But I couldn't call him on it, not now. Wouldn't matter anyway if Rainey turned out to be the man who'd strangled her.

The one thing that bothered me about that possibility was the blanket in the Crockett farmhouse. If the girl had been bestowing her favors on Rainey, why had they been meeting in such a place, all that distance from town? Why not do their trysting in the peddler's big, slab-sided wagon, down along the river someplace? And from what Jeb had told me, and that my own observations had confirmed, it wasn't that heavy wagon of Rainey's that'd mashed down the grass and weeds on the Crockett lane.

Axthelm said, "Where'd you take her?"

"Undertaking parlor in town."

"So the whole town knows by now."

"No, sir. The only ones who know are the ones I told you about and I swore them to secrecy. And Titus Bedford and Doc Olsen won't talk."

"It'll get out anyway."

"Maybe so, but not for a while with the lid on tight. Not until we can get a line on the man responsible, God willing."

"God willing. God don't care about the likes of us."

Wasn't anything I could say to that. "Have to ask you to make a positive identification when you come in to arrange for burial. Law requires it."

"Later today."

"Something else I have to ask," I said to break an awkward little silence. "Was your daughter keeping company with anyone in particular?"

"What's that mean, keeping company?"

"Seeing regular."

"No."

"Nobody she went out with more than once?"

"No."

"She must have had admirers—"

"Not that I know about."

I let it drop. There were other ways of finding out—Reba Purvis, for one, much as I disliked the prospect of asking her. "Well," I said. Then, "We'll find whoever did this thing and he'll hang for it, I promise you that."

There was another little silence before he said, "Anything more you want to know or say, Sheriff?"

"No, sir. Except my deepest sympathies to you and Mrs. Axthelm."

"Mine, too," Carse said, speaking for the first time.

A short, jerky nod, and Axthelm limped away to the house.

Carse drove us out of there. On our way through the gate, he said, "Seemed to me Mr. Axthelm was holding back on us." He's quick-witted, Carse is, doesn't miss much.

"Seemed that way to me, too. Plays his cards close to the vest."

"Kind of funny that he wouldn't know who she was stepping out with."

"She may not have had any callers at the ranch."

"Pretty young girl like her? Wouldn't he find that peculiar?"

"Not if he discouraged it. Or she pretended she wasn't interested in men, didn't want him to know who she was seeing."

"That business about her supposed to be up in Kalispell with her brother didn't sound right," Carse said. "You think maybe he found out someway about her and Rainey?"

"If he did, it'd have to be after Rainey pulled out."

"So Bob may not be in Kalispell, either. Axthelm could've sent him to find Rainey and fetch her back."

"Same thought crossed my mind."

So had another. Bob Axthelm was something of a hothead. If he had been sent on the peddler's trail and tracked him down, what would he do when he found out his sister wasn't with him?

SEVEN

IRST THING I did when we got back to town was to go
see Clyde Rademacher.

Clyde is Peaceful Valley's county attorney. He's also mayor
of Peaceful Bend and chairman of the board of education,
and if his wife, Ellie, has her way, he'll one day run for a seat
on the state legislature. He's a little on the pompous side,
Clyde, but I've called him a friend for twenty years. Best billiards player in the county when he sets his mind to it—next
to me, that is. We've had many a spirited game at the Commercial Club.

As county attorney he is responsible for summoning the
members of the coroner's jury as well as prosecuting criminals, so he had to be let in on the temporary secret about
the murder. So from the office I went to his big house on

Catalpa Street, a block and a half from where Reba lived. He and Ellie were home. Clyde Junior, the only one of their three offspring still living with them, was away somewhere, which made the telling easier than it might have been.

I could have insisted on a private talk with Clyde, but if I had, Ellie would've said something like "Clyde and I have no secrets from each other, Lucas, you know that. Go ahead and say what you've come to say." She's not as much of a busybody as Reba—cut from the same cloth, but she knows when to keep her mouth shut—and she rules the Rademacher roost. Besides, I had some questions for her. She was the take-charge sort elsewhere besides her home, one of her leadership roles being the organizing of church socials and the weekly dances at the community hall.

I kept the details of the crime and its discovery to the necessary minimum. The one thing I left out was my suspicions that Charity Axthelm had been carrying on with somebody in the abandoned farmhouse. Clyde didn't need to know it yet, and Ellie would have pounced on it the same as Reba would. It was still just speculation and I didn't want it to get out and spread around until if and when I found out if it had a bearing on the girl's murder.

They were both shocked at the news. Clyde shook his bald, knobby head and said, "Bad business, very bad. A blot on our community."

"I knew that man Rainey was a wastrel the first time I laid eyes on him," Ellie said.

"Woman chaser, do you mean?" I asked her.

"Yes. A sly charmer."

"Set out to take advantage of the Axthelm girl?"

"Of course he did, and obviously succeeded. She ran off
with him, didn't she? Or was planning to."

"You know that for a fact, Ellie?"

"Someone heard him bragging about it."

"Who?"

"I don't know. A reliable witness."

"According to who?"

"Reba Purvis."

Uh-huh, I thought.

Clyde said, "Do whatever is necessary to have him caught,
Lucas, before he seduces and destroys some other poor girl.
I'll see to it he's punished good and proper."

"If he's guilty."

"If? You have doubts?"

"Some. He doesn't seem to have much motive if Charity
was fixing to go away with him."

"Of course he does," Ellie said. "She must have changed
her mind at the last minute, and he flew into a rage and choked
the life out of her."

Out on the Crockett property? Why there, of all places?
But all I said was, "Maybe so."

"It *has* to be so. Who else could have done such a terrible
thing?"

"Well, I don't rightly know yet," I said. "The girl was pretty
and popular, must have had her share of swains. Any young
fellows in particular that you know about?"

Ellie has a long, narrow face, kind of horsey when she frowns and draws her mouth into a slash. "Surely you don't think one of our young men took her life?"

"I don't think anything at this point. Just exploring possibilities. *Was* she keeping company with anyone you know about?"

"No," she said, flat and kind of quick.

"Well, did she dance or spend time with one fella more than another?"

"I don't recall. She was . . . popular, as you said."

"Why the pause, Ellie?"

Now her mouth was set in prim lines. She didn't answer.

I said to prompt her, "I been told she had a reputation for being fast. Would you say it was deserved?"

"I have no way of knowing for certain. But I will say this: Where there's smoke there's fire. Yes, and what goes around comes around."

Clyde said, "Ellie, the poor girl has been brutally slain. No matter what her morals might have been, she didn't deserve to be murdered. Have some compassion."

"I do have compassion. I was merely answering Lucas's question."

This wasn't getting me anywhere, so I tried another tack. "What about girlfriends of hers? Anyone she was close enough to, to confide in?"

"Well . . . Laura Peabody, perhaps. I've seen them with their heads together a time or two."

Laura Peabody was a town girl. Lived with her folks on

the east edge, waited tables and did maid work at the Valley Hotel. As far as I knew, she didn't have Charity's kind of reputation and I wasn't about to ask Ellie for her opinion on the subject.

Clyde said he'd speak to Doc Olsen and Titus Bedford, and if they were in agreement, he'd set the coroner's jury meeting for Monday morning. I should have confided the poisoned buttermilk business to him before I left—probably would have if he and I had been alone—but Ellie was liable to set up a howl when she found out and start after me to arrest Grace Selkirk the way Reba had. To her mind, the attempted murder of a good friend held more weight than the actual murder of a youngster with dubious morals. I was in no frame of mind to put up with any more pressure, so as long as Reba kept her mouth shut I'd do the same for the time being.

THE WESTERN UNION office was over in the railroad depot. I went there next and had Bert Milbank send out wires to the law in the neighboring counties requesting that if James Rainey was found in their bailiwick, he be arrested and held for questioning. Wasn't much chance of Rainey still being in Peaceful Valley after three days or more, but it also wasn't likely he'd have traveled any long distance. His way of doing business seemed to be to spend two or three weeks in a particular area, trading with ranchers and farmers as well as townsfolk. That old red and green, slab-sided wagon of his was easy to spot, with JAMES RAINEY—FINE WARES, PATENT MED-ICINES, KNIVES SHARPENED FREE OF CHARGE painted large on both sides.

Doc was still at the mortuary, finishing up a more ex-tensive examination of Charity Axthelm's remains in the embalming room. Titus Bedford looked even more sorrow-ful and sad than he usually did when a fresh customer was brought in, but that didn't stop him from asking when Mr. and Mrs. Axthelm would be in to make arrangements. Titus has feelings for the bereaved, but he doesn't let them get in the way of his business sense. I told him what J.T. Axthelm had said. Then I asked him to make sure Grace Selkirk kept mum about the murder, and he said he would, that he'd already spoken to her about it.

I didn't care to see that poor girl's body stretched out on a slab, so I waited in the viewing room for Doc to come out. When he did, Titus left us alone without being asked.

"I stand by what I told you before, Lucas," Doc said. "Cause of death manual strangulation by a person with large, strong hands."

"Find any other marks on her body? Bruises or the like?"

"No. And no indication of sexual assault." He paused, sighed, and added, "This won't go into my report, but my professional opinion is that she wasn't a virgin."

"Uh-huh. What about her clothes? Anything on them that might help with the investigation?"

"Nothing as far as I could tell. Look at them yourself if you like."

"I'll do that. Anything else I should know, Doc?"

"No. At least not until I do an autopsy."

"When'll that be?"

"Tomorrow morning, after church," he said, and sighed again. "Grisly way to spend a Sunday."

I said, "I spoke to Clyde Rademacher. He'll arrange for the coroner's jury to meet here Monday morning."

"That'll do."

Doc went back into the embalming room to fetch the girl's clothing for me. I took the bundle to the sheriff's office. Carse was out somewhere, so I undertook the unpleasant chore of checking each garment myself. Gave me kind of a funny feeling to be handling the dead girl's torn and soiled clothing, but it had to be done.

I pricked my finger on something sharp that turned out to be a blackberry thorn. A couple more were stuck in the sheepskin coat, too, and there were tears in the cloth where other thorns had snagged it—all likely from the tangles by the old well when her body was carried out there. Wasn't anything else to find on the coat, dress, or underclothes. I wrapped everything up again, put the bundle in the safe, and went to scrub my hands with lye soap in the sink out back. Then I sat and did some studying on the button I'd found in the Crockett farmhouse.

Rust brown, with a couple of dangly same-color threads attached. Off the sleeve or front of a sack coat, I judged, that was neither brand new nor expensive. Wasn't dusty, so it hadn't lain under that old sofa for long. Ripped loose when the owner was in the act of strangling Charity Axthelm, maybe.

I tried to recall if James Rainey had worn such a coat. No, he hadn't, none of the times I'd seen him. Seemed to favor more casual garb: chambray shirts, corduroy trousers, cowhide jacket, Monkey Ward overcoat. Possible that he dressed up for his trysts, but it didn't strike me as likely. He wasn't the sort to bother spiffing himself to please or impress a pretty young girl. Handsome fella, slim and strong, with a brash and carefree line of patter; he didn't need any more than that to turn the head of a young girl, fast or not.

So if the button didn't belong to Rainey, who did it belong to? Had to be another of Charity Axthelm's lovers, whoever he was—a man who might also be her killer.

EIGHT

THE FIX MERCANTILE Company was on the corner of Main and Sycamore, a big, barnlike building with an attached storehouse at the rear. The store stocked as many different items as could be stuffed into both. Canned goods and dried fruits and wheels of cheese and barrels of crackers and pickles and other such items on one side, bolts of cloth and coats and hats and kitchen utensils and the like on the other; and out in the storehouse, shovels and pitchforks and buckets and kerosene, among many other things.

Weren't any customers when I walked in, just Tyler Fix sitting at the high desk behind the grocery counter. He's younger than his brother, Grover, by about eight years, and judging by his usual semi-sulky expression, he doesn't much care for being a storekeeper. Or could be he resents the fact that their father willed the mercantile to Grover alone. Elrod Fix evidently believed Tyler too young and irresponsible to share in the ownership, and he was probably right; Grover's smarter and more settled. He keeps Tyler in line, but you can see the kid chafing at the tether. I half expected to hear one of these days that he'd pulled up stakes and gone looking for a new and different pasture, if not necessarily a greener one.

Tyler mostly stocked shelves and made deliveries, that displeasured look of his not being conducive to good customer relations. Grover, on the other hand, was jovial and friendly and always aimed to please. The fact that it was late in the day was probably the reason Tyler was minding the store.

He said, "Sheriff," without much if any welcome as I stepped up to the counter. He was wearing a twin to the green eyeshade his brother always wore, but high on his forehead and set at an off-angle on his mop of curly red hair. Maybe he thought he cut a jaunty figure; to me, it just looked foolish. "Just about to close up."

"I won't be here long. Grover off to home?"

"No, he's here. Doing something out in the storehouse."

"Mind fetching him?"

I could see it in Tyler to make a smart-aleck remark, but the look in my eye convinced him otherwise. He said, "Guess not," and got up, taking his time, and ambled to the covered aisle at the rear that led to the storehouse.

I went over to the rack of men's wear. None of the coats on display was the same rust-brown color as the button I'd found.

Tyler came back in with Grover, who was a couple of

inches taller, his red hair not as long or as curly. "Always a pleasure, Sheriff Monk. What can I do for you?"

I showed him the button with its dangly threads. "This look familiar to you?"

He peered at it. "Came off a sack coat, I'd say."

"Uh-huh. You stock any this color?"

"None right now. Seems to me we did at one time."

"Recall who might've bought one?"

"Well . . . no," Grover said. "You, Brother?"

Tyler fingered the mustache he was trying to grow, a wispy little thing with no more than a dozen short hairs. "No. I don't think we ever had one exactly that color."

I said, "Either of you notice anyone wearing one like this recently?"

Tyler said, "Not that I remember."

"Grover?"

He shook his head.

"Well, if anything comes to mind, give me a holler."

"Important, is it?" Grover asked.

"Might be. Just might be."

When I left the mercantile, I thought about stopping at the Commercial Club and showing the button around in there. The Commercial is one of the social hubs of Peaceful Bend and draws men young and old of all types and stations, me among them, who like to shoot pool and billiards, play cribbage or pinochle or rummy, and hobnob in quiet surroundings. But it was late afternoon, lull time at the club. Even the old farts who made up the Hot Stove League, gathering to gossip and tell tall tales and trade off-color stories, would've left by now, looking to work up an appetite for supper in one of the saloons.

I went to the Valley Hotel instead.

Supper service had already started in the dining room, but it was too early for much business. Only one table was occupied—two after I pulled up a chair on the opposite side of the room. Laura Peabody, wearing her pink-and-white waitress outfit, had been idling by the coffee bar; she came straight over to me. She was a little on the plump side, with taffy-colored hair, a perky manner, and a smile that lit her face up like a lamp.

"Two specials tonight, Sheriff," she said. "Stew and dumplings and roast pork loin. No oysters yet."

"Just coffee'll do me, thanks." When she brought it, I said, "Sit with me a minute, Laura. You're not busy and there's something I need to talk to you about."

"Well . . . I guess it'll be okay." She sat down, but with her chair pulled back in case she was called or more customers came in. "I haven't done anything wrong, have I?"

"Not that I know about. I understand you're a friend of Charity Axthelm."

"Charity?" Her smile wobbled some. "We're not exactly friends. I mean, not real close friends."

"She tell you about her plans with James Rainey?"

"Oh, my. You know about that?"

"So she did tell you."

Laura shifted around in her chair; the smile was gone now. "Yes, she told me. I tried to talk her out of going away with him, but she said she loved him, really loved him, and he loved her."

"She feel that way about anybody before Rainey?"

"In love, you mean?" Spots of color appeared on the girl's cheeks. "I guess she must have."

"Who with?"

"Well . . . I don't know as I should be telling tales . . ."

"You won't be. Just cooperating, is all."

"Is something wrong, Sheriff? Has something happened?"

I said, gentle, "Who were her other admirers, Laura?"

"I can't say for sure. I mean, Charity . . . well, she could be kind of secretive about things like that. But I know she was seeing Devlin Stonehouse at one time."

I knew Devlin slightly; he worked as a teller at the Merchant's Bank. "Serious between them?"

"I don't know what you mean by serious."

Well, I couldn't come right out and ask if she knew or suspected that they'd been making the beast with two backs, so I just said, "Stepping out together regular."

"No more so than with any of her other beaux, I guess."

"Other beaux such as who?"

"Well . . ." Her voice had been low; she lowered it even more when she said, "Clyde Rademacher. Clyde Junior, I mean."

That raised my eyebrows. Shouldn't have, I guess. Clyde Junior was a strapping specimen, unattached and no less prone to sow a batch of wild oats than any other fella his age. Maybe Ellie Rademacher had been so quick to say no because she knew her son was one of the Axthelm girl's admirers and didn't want me getting the wrong idea. Be just like a mother hen like her to protect one of her brood.

"Anybody else?"

"I don't understand, Sheriff Monk. What does it matter who was interested in Charity before she went off with James Rainey?"

"I don't know that it does," I said. "*Was* there anybody else?"

Laura took a nibble on her lower lip and the color spots darkened a mite. But just then two more people came into the dining room. She hopped up quick, a little too quick. "I've tarried long enough. Mr. Coombs gets angry if he thinks I'm shirking."

"Answer the question before you go."

Seemed to me there was a hesitation before she said, "No. Nobody else I know about."

NINE

THE BANK IS closed Saturdays, and would be closed at this hour anyway, so I set off to Ruth Hollings's boardinghouse, where I'd heard Devlin Stonehouse had a room. He did, but he wasn't in it, and Mrs. Hollings didn't know when he would be or where I could find him. That left a conversation with Clyde Junior, but like as not he'd be home for supper about now and I wasn't going to question him about Charity Axthelm with his father and mother present. He and Devlin could both wait until tomorrow.

It was well past six o'clock now. Since I lost Tess, my evenings tend to be pretty quiet and of a sameness, and this one started out as more of the same. Supper in the Elite Café, then on to my house on State Street, where I fed and walked

Butch, the old, half-blind mongrel dog I've had for a dozen years. After that, most nights, I'd do such other chores as needed doing, turn in, and read myself to sleep. Gets lonely sometimes, especially around the holidays—Butch has gotten grumpy in his dotage, developed a tendency to pass gas awake and asleep both, and isn't much of a companion anymore—but a man learns to live with that, same as he learns to live with all the other things, good and bad, that make up his life.

This night, I sat down to write a letter to my daughter, Katherine, in Bozeman. She went there two years ago to take some courses at Montana State University—whip-smart, that girl of mine—and ended up marrying a nice young fella named Jim Firebaugh who was studying to be a mining engineer. Invited me down to attend the wedding, which made me even prouder of her than I already was. Likewise the fact that she stayed in school, too, after the nuptials.

A year and a half had passed now and her and Jim hadn't yet presented me with a grandchild, but I had no doubt they'd work on it eventually if they weren't already. Katherine takes after her mother, which is to say she's never been shy and is bound to be as red-blooded as Tess was; I caught her once when she was sixteen reading a how-to book on marital relations she'd got hold of somewhere.

I was halfway through the letter when somebody started whacking the knocker on my front door. Better not be Reba, I thought, come to harass me some more. It wasn't. The caller was Sam Prine.

"Sorry to bother you, Sheriff," he said, "but I figured you'd want to know. There's trouble brewing over at Monahan's."

"What kind of trouble?"

"The anti-Indian kind. Henry Bandelier's stirring it up with loose talk to anybody who'll listen."

So Bandelier had ignored my warning and was as much as spitting in my eye. Blasted fool was born without the sense God gave a picket-pin gopher. "Drunk talk?"

"About half and half. He wasn't drunk enough or loud enough so's I could arrest him for disturbing the peace."

"Saying what about the Indians?"

"Calling 'em war-whoop heathens and low-down thieves. Taking your name in vain, too, for not arresting Tom Black Wolf and Charlie Walks Far."

"How many hotheads has he got feeling the way he does?"

"Not too many when I left," Sam said. "Four or five that think the way he does."

Enough to cause a ruckus if Bandelier got 'em riled enough to bunch up and head out to the reservation. There hadn't been any trouble to speak of with the Indians in a long while, but if he succeeded in creating some, red men and white both would end up getting hurt. And all on account of a dadblamed hunk of junk.

I went and got my hat and coat, and Sam and I made tracks for Monahan's. It was the least of the four watering holes in Peaceful Bend, not in the town proper but on Douglas Street over by the railroad tracks. One-third saloon, one-third poker parlor and pool hall, and one-third sporting house that catered to railroad workers, ranch and farm hands, and such riffraff as drifted through. Most of the fights Sam had to break up and drunks he had to arrest were Monahan's customers.

The Ladies Aid Society, with Reba in the forefront, kept trying to convince me and the town council to close down the part she called "the den of iniquity inhabited by fallen women," if not the entire place, but I never was a believer in trying to legislate morals. Regulating prostitution and gambling so they didn't get out of hand, yes—I kept a sharp eye on Monahan's and the handful of other resorts in Peaceful Valley—but so long as Pete Monahan kept his bar girls in line and clean of social disease, I saw no reason to shut him down and neither did the town council or the county commissioners. Nor the majority of voters, for that matter.

Monahan's was a broad, two-story frame building lit up bright and rackety tonight with piano music and loud voices. But the piano man quit playing and the customers quieted down some when Sam and I walked in, the way it always happens when a couple of lawmen come into a saloon unexpectedly. The place was doing its usual heavy Saturday night business, full up at the bar, all of the tables and poker and faro layouts occupied, the two inches of sawdust spread over the floor already thick-littered with cigar and cigarette butts. I counted three bar girls wearing red dresses and come-hither smiles; the rest were either in the poolroom at the back or upstairs entertaining. None of the customers here was Henry Bandelier.

"Where was Bandelier rabble-rousing, Sam? Poolroom?"

"Yep."

"He'd better still be there."

The poolroom was beyond the staircase to the upper floor, through a narrow archway and down a short corridor. Even though the piano had started racketing again, I could hear Bandelier's loud voice as soon as we stepped through the archway. I wanted an earful of what he was saying before we went in, so I made a gesture to Sam and we eased up to where I could sneak a look through a second narrow archway into the big room.

I counted eight men, half I knew by name, gathered around the two beat-up pool tables, their attention hard-focused on Bandelier. He was over in front of the rack of cues and chalk, red-faced with drink and bile, a Cuba Libre pan-atela in one hand and a ditchwater highball, the Montana tip-pler's favorite drink, in the other. I don't know what it is about little men like him—feelings of inferiority and inadequacy on account of their size, I suppose—but once they take over the floor, they seem to grow about six inches and stand high in the collar, at least in their own minds.

"You mark my words," he was declaiming in a not quite slurred voice. "If we let young bucks like Black Wolf and Walks Far get away with thievery, there'll be other renegades that follow suit. Won't be property belonging to any of us that's safe."

"Our womanfolk, neither," another damn fool said. Buster Grimes, a long-jawed stablehand on one of the ranches.

"That's right, our womenfolk, either."

That little exchange would have been a touch humorous

if it wasn't so serious. Neither Grimes nor Bandelier was married.

"Those war-whoop heathens need to be taught a lesson, a hard lesson. If Sheriff Monk won't make them tell what they did with my statue, I say we do it ourselves."

"I dunno, Mr. Bandelier. That old coot Monk's dead set against vigilantes." That was Virgil Tyree, seasonal worker, moocher, and nickel-nurser when he had a nickel to nurse.

"I'm not talking vigilantes. Just a . . . kind of unofficial posse comitatus." He waved his cigar and swallowed some whiskey and water for emphasis. "Put on a show of force to get my property back and let those Indians know they better not try any more stealing or they'll regret it. Them and any other bucks that try doing what they did."

"Put the fear of God into 'em." A belly-fat yahoo I didn't know, maybe a railroad section hand from the way he was dressed.

"That's right. Give them a scare they'll never forget."

"Suppose they put up a fight?" Young Jack Vanner, carpenter's apprentice and part-time handyman. "Then what? Beat the truth out of them?"

"It won't come to that," Bandelier said. "There won't be any need for violence."

"Suppose they start some?"

"They won't. But if they do, why, we'll just have to finish it, that's all."

Tyree: "When do we go? Tonight?"

Vanner: "Maybe we ought to wait a day or two, give the sheriff another chance to do his job."

Bandelier, around the jut of his cigar: "I don't see any reason to wait. Monk's had two days to get my property back and being the Indian lover he is, it's likely he never will. I say we ride out to the reservation right now!"

That was enough for me. More than enough. I stepped out and into the room and said in a tolerable roar, "Like hell you will!"

They all jerked and jumped and Bandelier near choked on his cigar smoke. One long look at me and Sam and he wasn't standing tall anymore. You could almost see him shrink down small again.

"I've seen horse manure laid out thick before," I said, hard, "but none thicker nor smellier than what you've been spreading, Henry. I ought to put you in handcuffs and haul you off to jail."

"Arrest me? On what charge?"

"Charges. Drunk and disorderly. Disturbing the peace. Inciting an illegal trespass on government land for the purpose of malicious mischief—"

"I'm not drunk and I'm not disturbing the peace!"

"—and anything else I can think of. Impersonating a duly elected officer of the law, maybe."

"What? I did no such thing."

"The same as, with that 'posse comitatus' remark of yours."

"What're you talking about?"

"There isn't any such thing as an unofficial posse comitatus; only the county sheriff has the power to organize an official one in order to pursue and arrest a felon or felons. You claiming you can assume that power amounts to imperson-ation." I looked at Sam Prine. "That the way you see it, Sam?"

"Sure do," he agreed.

Bandelier commenced to sputter and whine about only wanting his stolen statue found and returned.

"Henry," I said, "you know what's good for you, you won't give me any more guff on that subject."

Virgil Tyree said, "Now look here, Sheriff, you got no call to— Uuhh!"

The grunt was because I stepped up and jabbed two stiff-ened fingers under his wishbone, hard enough to stagger him backward a step. "That's for calling me an old coot. Say it again and you'll find yourself on the floor with my foot in your ass and your face in a spittoon."

That took the starch out of him quick enough. Bandelier and the others, too. None of 'em had anything more to say, nor would they look me in the eye straight on.

I said to Bandelier, "Now listen good. I reckon I'll let you off the hook this time, but if I hear any more about taking the law into your own hands, or making trouble for the Indi-ans, I will charge you and lock you up. That goes for the rest of you knotheads, too. Understood?"

Chin dips and sullen looks.

"All right. Get on out of here, go home where you belong."

They didn't waste any time obeying the order. In less than ten seconds, Sam Prine and I were alone in the room.

"By grab, Lucas, you sure can be a feisty booger when you get your back up."

He said it in an admiring kind of way so I didn't take offense. Besides, he was right, I *can* be a feisty booger. It takes a fair lot to make me mad, but when it happens, them that's responsible are in for a hard time.

TEN

WHEN TESS WAS alive, she dragged me to church every Sunday unless I could find a good excuse not to go. Now, it's Reba who keeps trying to make less of a sinner out of me, but she's easier to resist than Tess was. Good thing she didn't come around badgering me this Sunday morning. With all that was gnawing on my mind, the last thing I needed was to hear one of Reverend Noakes's sermons, which were either the fire-and-brimstone sort—he seemed to think just about everybody in Peaceful Bend was an unrepentant defiler of the Ten Commandments—or the repetitious love-thy-neighbor-or-else sort that he delivered in the same thunderous voice. It's not that I'm an unbeliever, it's just that I think a man ought to be allowed to practice his religious beliefs in private, without having his ears blistered in public.

I finished my letter to Katherine, not mentioning either the murder or the attempted murder, and posted it on my way to the Western Union office. Weren't any responses to my wires; wherever James Rainey was, he hadn't been spotted and taken into custody yet. The sheriff's office is closed on Sundays except when there's an emergency, so I didn't bother going there. Or yet to the Bedford Funeral Parlor where Doc Olsen was doing his coroner's duty. I looked in on an autopsy once, my first term in office, and that once was more than enough.

There was no buzz among the folks I passed and said good morning to on Main Street, or in the Elite Café where I ate my usual Sunday breakfast of sausages and buckwheat pancakes, so the news about Charity Axthelm hadn't leaked out yet. A wonder that Reba and her gossip-sniffing nose hadn't caught a whiff of it by now, nor anybody else had. Well, as Reverend Noakes was fond of saying, God works in mysterious ways.

I didn't much feel like facing Reba again, but I figured I might as well get it over with. She'd be sure to start in on me again about arresting Grace Selkirk, evidence or no evidence. If I could deflect that business long enough to get her to talk about Charity Axthelm's immorality and involvement with James Rainey, she'd gladly reveal all she knew or suspected. I'd just have to be careful in how I broached the subject so she wouldn't get a hint of why I was interested.

Only problem was, Reba wasn't home. My twist of the doorbell was answered by Hannah Mead.

"Reba went to a luncheon after church," she said. "I don't know when she'll be back."

"I'll catch her later. It's good to see you up and around, Hannah."

"I'm still feeling poorly," she said. Looked it, too. Pale, damp-cheeked, a kind of dull sheen to her eyes, her big-boned body slumped against the doorframe. "But I can't keep lying abed like a invalid."

"Mind answering a few questions while I'm here?"

"About the buttermilk? I don't know anything. Reba thinks it was Grace Selkirk who poisoned it."

"I know. Just a few questions, Hannah."

She let me in and we went into the parlor. She'd been sit-ting in a walnut rocker, crocheting something or other; she sat down there again, draped a shawl over her lap, and picked up her crochet bag.

I said, "Reba told me she caught Grace Selkirk spying on the house a couple of days ago and they had words about it."

"Yes. She was real upset."

"Did you see them arguing?"

"No. I mind my own business."

"See the Selkirk woman at all that day?"

"On the street as I was coming back from shopping. First time I ever had a good look at her."

"How'd you know who she was?"

"Reba talked about her, said what she looked like." Han-nah paused, her crochet hook poised in one hand. "Funny thing," she said then.

"What was?"

"You hear somebody talked about and you get a picture in your mind. But then you see them in the flesh, up close, and the picture's not quite the same. You know what I mean, Sheriff?"

"I do."

"Well, I didn't get a real good look at Grace Selkirk, but she reminded me of somebody."

"Somebody you used to know?"

"I'm not sure. I can't quite place who or where."

"You think she might've had the same feeling?"

"I can't say. She turned her head away kind of quick when we passed."

"And you didn't see her again that day?"

"Again? No."

"You tell Reba about this?"

Hannah's head was still paining her; the waggle she gave it brought on a wince. "Should I have?"

"No, and don't trouble her with it. Try to remember who Grace Selkirk reminded you of, and if you do, call me up or come tell me."

"I will. It'll come to me when my thinking is clear again— my head still feels like it's stuffed full of cotton. But I don't see why it's important."

Probably wasn't. But then again, the way my mind works, there was a chance it could be.

DEVLIN STONEHOUSE SAID, "I was taken with Charity, yes. Danced with her every chance I had, bought her a ticket to

the Chautauqua last summer, but that was as far as our so-
cializing went. She wasn't interested in me the way I was in
her. Turned me down when I asked to call on her, take her
riding and on a picnic."

He sounded wistful and maybe a touch bitter. Good-
looking young fella, dark-haired, clean-shaven, probably not
used to being rejected by pretty girls. But he was sober-
sided and serious about his job at the bank—apparently
not carefree and fun-loving enough for a girl like Charity
Axthelm.

"You happen to know of anyone she didn't turn down?"

"That traveling peddler, Rainey, obviously." The words
came out disapproving and more than a touch bitter. "I still
can't believe she would take up and then run off with a man
like that."

"When did you hear about it?"

"Two days ago, after they'd already gone."

"Uh-huh. She didn't strike you as the sort for rash behavior?"

"Not that kind, no."

"Some other kind?"

He clamped his lips together and looked off into the
cold blue sky. We were on the front porch of Ruth Hollings's
boardinghouse, sitting in a couple of her padded chairs. He
was still dressed for church, in a dark suit and a bow tie with
little gold stars on it.

"Some other kind, Devlin?" I asked again.

"I'd rather not say. She made a fool of herself and now
she's gone, that's all that matters."

No, it wasn't. What mattered was who'd choked the life out of her and dumped her body down that well. "Some folks say she had a reputation for being fast. Any truth to it, far as you know?"

"Some folks ought to mind their own business."

"No argument there. But I'm not paid to be one of them."

He said, frowning, "Do all these questions have something to do with her and Rainey?"

"They might. I'd appreciate an answer."

It took a few seconds for him to say, "There was talk, yes. If it was true, then God help her. But I didn't pay any attention to it. That was not why I was interested in her."

"Who was interested for that reason? Anybody you know of?"

"No one bragging to me, if that's what you mean."

"Put it this way, then. Fellas she didn't turn down when she was asked to go riding or picnicking."

"What does that have to do with her and Rainey?"

"Reluctant to say? It's just between you and me."

". . . All right. Clyde Rademacher. Clyde Junior. She was seeing a lot of him."

"When?"

"Late spring, early summer."

"But not right before Rainey showed up?"

"I don't think so."

"Who was she seeing then?"

"I'd tell you if I knew, but I don't. She didn't talk about it. She could be . . . secretive about her personal life."

"Nobody else talked about it? None of her admirers?"

"Not as far as I know. Nobody ever said a word to me."

Stonehouse sounded kind of bitter about that, too. As sober-sided and censorious as he was, I had the idea that not too many his age, male or female, confided in him about much of anything of a private nature.

It was past noon by then. I put off hunting for Clyde Junior in favor of a visit to the undertaking parlor to find out if Doc Olsen was finished with his carving.

He was. Just washing up, Titus told me. I asked him if Charity's folks had come in yesterday, and he said they had. The family didn't want a funeral or burial in the town cemetery, their aim being to claim the girl's shell once it was officially released and lay her to rest on their own property. Titus's expression said he didn't approve, but it was their privilege. No law against it.

Grace Selkirk was out of sight and earshot in the sewing room, so while I had Titus alone I asked him if he had any idea where the woman had lived before coming to Peaceful Bend or why she'd picked our town to settle in. No, he didn't. She'd been closemouthed about her past and he hadn't wanted to pry. About all she'd told him was that she had past experience at sewing, and proved it by the expert way she trimmed coffins.

"Grace told me about the poisoned buttermilk," Titus said then. "I made her promise not to give even a hint to anybody else."

"Good."

"You don't still suspicion she was responsible?"

"My mind's open on the subject," I said. "You know her better than I do. Would you say she's capable of it?"

"I don't like to think anybody's capable of a terrible thing like that. Especially a woman who lives in my house and works for me."

"I need to ask a personal question, Titus. You don't have to answer it, and if you tell me to go to the devil I won't hold it against you."

"Go ahead and ask."

"There anything between you and Grace Selkirk?"

A corner of his mouth twitched. "You mean am I sleeping with her? No."

"She ever issue an invitation, straight out or otherwise?"

"That makes two questions."

"I know it, and it's the last I'll ask. Did she?"

He scratched at his side-whiskers before he said, "Once. And no, she wasn't upset when I declined. Neither of us has spoken of it since." The way he said that, with a little side-shift of his eyes, made me wonder if he regretted passing up the opportunity, or if he truly had passed it up. Titus is a moral gent, not given to telling lies, but every man has his weaknesses. Tempt a fellow often enough and just right and he'd be hard-pressed not to let his halo slip down a notch or two.

Anyhow, Grace Selkirk had lied to me about having no personal interest in him. Seemed likely enough that Reba was right and the woman wanted more than just a roof over her head and a few dollars' pay. One lie didn't make her guilty of attempted murder, but it did supply her with a motive if she was after Titus and his money and believed Reba was a rival. Still a pretty thin one, though. I wished I knew more about the woman. More reason to hope Hannah Mead remembered who Grace Selkirk reminded her of.

Doc Olsen came out just then, Sunday-dressed, his long face set in mournful lines. When he saw me he said, "Good, you're here. Saves me from having to hunt for you." He took hold of my arm. "Come on, we'll talk outside. Excuse us, Titus."

We went on out. Through the plate-glass show window, I could see Grace Selkirk working at trimming another coffin. Charity Axthelm's coffin? I didn't like to think that it was.

Doc steered me over to the driveway where his Tin Lizzie was parked. "Autopsy's finished," he said. "Grisly work for a Sunday."

"You said that yesterday."

"And I'll probably say it again to somebody else."

"Official cause of death still what you figured it was?"

"Yes. Manual strangulation."

"Could you get a reasonable fix on the time of death?"

"Best estimate is sometime Thursday evening. I can't pin it down any closer than that."

"Anything else I should know?"

"Yes, dammit," Doc said. "The girl was pregnant. Five to six weeks along."

ELEVEN

I WAS ON my way to the Commercial Club—nobody home
at the Rademachers, wouldn't you know—when Bert Milbank came hurrying up.

"Telegram just come for you, Sheriff. Thought you'd want
to see it right away."

"Good man. Thanks."

I tore open the envelope. The wire was from the law in
Timber Point, the Ridgely County seat over on the Clark's
Fork northeast of Missoula.

JAMES RAINEY HERE STOP BADLY INJURED
UNABLE TO ARREST YET STOP ADVISE STOP
                              T. BANNERMAN
                              SHERIFF

Hell's bells! T. Bannerman was newly elected; I didn't know him, never had any dealings before. He was either narrow between the ears or a pinchpenny with the county taxpayers' money. "Badly injured" meaning what? How badly? How injured?

Bert had stayed hovering while I read. "You want to send a reply?" he asked.

"Damn tootin' I do."

I went with him back to his office at the depot, where I wrote crisp to T. Bannerman requesting further details and asking if Rainey was in a condition to answer questions. And made the last word in the message URGENT so if he was any kind of lawman, he wouldn't dawdle.

"Bring his reply to the sheriff's office, Bert, soon as you get it."

"Sure thing, but I'm off duty at six. Comes in after that, where should I tell the night man to bring it?"

"My office first, if I'm not there then my house."

I hurried on to the Commercial Club. Being a bachelor, Carse spends most of his Sunday afternoons there playing pitch or cribbage with his cronies, and honing his card skills with beer. Which is what he was doing today, and he hadn't had enough suds to fuzz his thinking. I rousted him away from the crib board, and waited until we were outside and clear of earshot before I told him why.

"Rainey's in Timber Point, laid up with some kind of injuries," I said. "Pisshawk new sheriff over there didn't provide any more information, so now we have to wait on another wire from him. If Rainey's in shape to talk, one of us'll have to question him."

"Me?"

"You. Plenty to keep me busy here, not the least of which is testifying to the coroner's jury. You don't mind, do you?"

"Round-trip train ride to Missoula, round-trip stage or horse ride to Timber Point if there's no train service twixt the two. And there isn't yet, as I recollect. Why should I mind?" His tone was mild. One thing Carse isn't, it's a complainer. "Leave today or in the morning?"

"Early morning's soon enough. If it turns out necessary."

"Okay."

"There's something else you better know," I said. "I saw Doc Olsen over at Bedford's after he finished his autopsy. The Axthelm girl was pregnant."

"Oh, Lordy. How far along?"

"Five to six weeks."

"That lets out Rainey."

"As the father, likely so. But it doesn't let him out as the son of a bitch who strangled her."

"Could be she told him she was in a family way by some-body else and he jumped up in the collar and killed her."

"Could be," I agreed. "But it doesn't explain what they were doing on the Crockett property."

"What she hadn't ought to've been," Carse said, wry.

"We been over that. No need for her and Rainey to meet out there, when he had that closed-in wagon of his. And no tracks deep enough on the lane for the wagon to've made."

"So you're thinking she might've been killed by the man who seeded her. On account of he found out she was running off with Rainey?"

"Not thinking anything yet," I said. "Just playing wait and see." But it seemed to fit together better that way. We'd have a better idea after Carse questioned Rainey, if such were possible right away.

I sent Carse down to the courthouse to wait on further word from T. Bannerman, and walked myself back over to the Rademachers. This time I got lucky, if you could call it that. I was about to cross the street when a machine racketed around the near corner, traveling about five miles over the speed limit and toting a raggedy trail of dust behind. It was Clyde Rademacher's year-old KRIT Touring automobile, bought from a salesman in Missoula, as were most of the machines in the valley, including my Model T. Clyde Junior was at the wheel, a pair of goggles over his eyes that gave him the look of a giant bug. He waggled a hand at me in passing, but he didn't slow down until he got to the driveway that led back to the carriage barn behind their house.

I went on over there and waited for him to show himself afoot. He was the spitting image of his father, except that he had a full head of sandy hair and a darker skin color on account of he'd spent the summer and most of the fall working outdoors on the Bruderstein hay ranch. His folks despaired of him for not wanting to go to college, study law, and join Clyde in his firm. He was brash and a touch wild, but you had to give him credit for being his own man, following his own plans for his future, whatever they happened to be.

He hadn't made his intentions clear, maybe because he didn't know himself yet just what they were.

He was wearing a duster and one of his wide, cheeky grins. "Afternoon, Mr. Monk." He always called me Mr. Monk, which would have been nice and polite except that, intentional or not, he managed to give the "mister" a faint mocking emphasis.

I said, "By rights I ought to give you a citation."

"Citation? What for?"

"Exceeding the town speed limit."

"Didn't realize I was."

"Should have. You could've run down a kid or a dog."

"But I didn't. I always pay close attention to my driving."

"Uh-huh. Well, pay closer attention to the speed limit next time."

"I'll do that," he said. "The folks aren't home, Mr. Monk. They were invited out to supper at the Weldons."

"It's you I come to see."

"Oh? What can I do for you?"

"Tell me about you and Charity Axthelm." No point in mincing words.

The cheeky grin didn't waver. "I hear she ran off with that traveling peddler, Rainey. Nothing to do with me."

"I been told you kept company with her at one time."

"At one time. I keep company with a lot of girls."

"When, exactly, with her?"

"Back in the spring."

"For how long?"

"Not long. Month or so."

"What busted up the romance?"

"Romance?" He laughed. "I wouldn't call it that."

"What would you call it?"

"Why do you want to know?"

"Never mind why. If it wasn't a romance, what was it?"

"Opportunity realized, you might say."

"Meaning what? Speak plain, boy."

"Well, what do you suppose it means?" he said. "She had something we both wanted at the time. Sort of took advantage of each other, you might say."

"Uh-huh. You had relations with her."

"What if I did? You fixing to tell my folks?"

"No." Not unless I had to. "Just between us."

"Okay, then, I did. I wasn't the first, and I sure wasn't the last. And that's not telling tales, now she's gone and not likely to return."

Clyde Junior didn't know how right he was. Or maybe he did, though I hoped not. If he didn't know, he'd find out soon enough—but not from me, not now.

"How long since the last time you and her were together?"

"I told you. Last spring."

"Nothing to do with her since?"

"Nothing at all."

"Where'd you do your sporting? One of the abandoned farms, maybe?"

Maybe he thought the word "sporting" was funny; he laughed again. "No need, when you've got a motorcar and there's plenty of private places by the river to park."

Clyde Junior was beginning to get under my skin. Too damn cocksure for his own good, much less mine. "Who else had relations with her?"

"You don't think she'd tell me? She didn't."

"I was young once," I said. "Kids your age brag often enough."

That last statement bristled him, as I meant it to. The annoying grin flickered and thinned. "I'm not a kid, I'm a grown man."

"Then act like one. Who else?"

"Half the men in town under the age of thirty, probably."

"I had just about enough of your smart-ass," I said, sharp. "Answer my question and answer it proper."

He said, "All right," his voice a little sulky now. "I only know of one for sure. Besides the peddler."

"Name him."

"Jack Vanner."

Well, now. Vanner was the rowdy type; Sam Prine had locked him up once for attacking another man in Monahan's with a broken chair leg. Indian hater, too, as his presence at Henry Bandelier's attempted rabble-rousing last night pointed out. Not the sort I'd have associated with Charity Axthelm. But then, you can never tell about women's tastes in men. Takes variety in temperament as well as looks to satisfy some.

"How do you know that?" I asked.

"He boasted to me, half drunk, one night while I was seeing her. I knocked him on his ass."

"Boasts can be plain lies."

"Not his. Only way he could've known about a mole she has. Want to know where?"

"No."

I showed him the rust-brown button. No reaction when he looked at it, not even an eyeflick. "Ever see Vanner wearing a coat this color, with buttons like this?"

"Not his sort of garb. Why?"

"Never mind why. Know anybody who wears one?"

"No."

"Who else was seeing Charity besides you and Vanner?"

"Don't forget the peddler."

"I'm not forgetting him. Any others?"

"None that I know about." Clyde Junior cocked his head forward like a bird dog about to point. "I sure wish you'd tell me how come you're so interested in Charity and her doings."

I said, "I'll bet you do," and left him standing there with his mouth half open as if he was about to swallow what was left of his grin.

JACK VANNER HAD a room above Otis Moore's carpentry shop. But he wasn't in it and the shop was closed up tight. He might be over at Monahan's, but if so, it'd be a mistake to brace him in front of his rowdy sidekicks. And if he wasn't there, it was too cold and blustery with the afternoon on the wane to go hunting his whereabouts. Words with him could wait until tomorrow.

I hied myself to the courthouse. I expected Carse to be alone in the office, but he wasn't. He had company, and none too pleasant company from the scowly look on the visitor's face.

Bob Axthelm was back home in Peaceful Valley.

TWELVE

YOUNG AXTHELM HADN'T been there very long. He was on his feet, his rawboned frame bent forward and one big-knuckled, hairy-backed hand braced on a corner of Carse's desk. Carse sat stiff in his chair, the copy of *Adventure* he'd had his nose in when he was interrupted tented open in front of him. Judging by what he was saying when I came in, he'd been getting an earful of something he didn't much like.

"You got no call to bullyrag me, son. Sheriff's doing all he can."

"Sure he is," Bob Axthelm said. "You, too, sitting here on your ass."

Then he saw me and straightened up, hitching at the belt of his worn Levi's. He thrust his head in my direction, the cords in his long neck stretched rope-tight. Pretty upset, all right. I didn't blame him for that, but Carse was right, he had no call to come bullyragging.

I said, "Simmer down, Bob, settle your hocks. We're not shirking or lollygagging, neither of us. Investigations take time—"

"Time! My sister's been dead four days."

"Yes, but she was only found yesterday. Word hasn't gotten out yet, and we're being careful it doesn't until the coroner's jury convenes on Monday."

"To hell with the coroner's jury. Don't need them to tell who choked her to death."

I shed my mackinaw, hung it and my derby on the coatrack. Instead of sitting, I cocked a hip on the front edge of my desk. Bob Axthelm stayed upright.

"Who do you reckon is the guilty man?" I asked him.

"Who else but that peddler Rainey. Charity was set to run off with him, you know that."

"We know it. How'd you find it out?"

"That don't matter. Why aren't you and your deputy out hunting the son of a bitch?"

"No need. We know where Rainey is. What we don't know yet is whether or not he's a murderer."

The boy's upper lip lifted high to show his teeth and gums, the way a dog's does when it's riled and snarly. "Who the hell else. Where is he?"

"Where we can get to him. And will, tomorrow."

"Tomorrow doesn't satisfy, Sheriff. Where?"

"Maybe you've got an idea where."

"Hell. How would I?"

I said, mild, "Where've you been the past few days?"

"What kind of question is that?"

"One that can use an answer."

"Pa told you where I've been. Kalispell."

"How'd you get those scrapes and bruises on your knuckles?"

"What?"

"You heard me. Simple question. Must've been recent—they look pretty fresh."

He shied a look at his hand, then rubbed the sore spots. His scowl was dark as a rain cloud. "None of your business."

"It is if how you got them involves Rainey."

"I don't know what you're talking about."

"We been told Rainey's hurt, bad hurt."

"Yeah? How bad?"

"Don't know yet. We're waiting on further word. Could be somebody beat up on him."

"And you think it might've been me? Well, it wasn't. I'd've hammered the crap out of him if I'd caught him messing with Charity, no use denying that, but I only set eyes on him once and that was here in town."

"Did you know she was set on going away with him?"

"Not until I got back this morning and Pa told me."

"How'd he find out?"

"If he didn't tell you, then why should I?"

"Could be he went looking for Rainey, to bring your sister back home if he thought she was with him."

"Well, he didn't."

"How do you know he didn't?"

"I know Pa, that's how. He ain't made that way."

"Are you?"

No answer.

I said, "I'll ask you again, Bob. How'd your pa find out?"

Young Axthelm chewed on the question, scrunch-faced as if it were a wad of something with a bad taste. Then, as if spitting it out, "Ma told him."

"Charity told her, is that it?"

"No," he said, bitter, "one of our nosy neighbors come by and told her. Heard the gossip in town and wanted to know was it true. Until then her and Pa thought Charity'd gone to Kalispell with me."

That cleared up that part of things. Or it did if Bob was telling the whole truth. I said, "All right, then. So you and your folks didn't know she was seeing Rainey on the sly. Was she seeing anybody else you know about?"

"Don't matter if she was."

"It might if Rainey's innocent."

"Innocent! Christ!"

"If he is," I said, "then somebody else is guilty. Somebody right here in the valley."

His face scrunched up again. "Ain't no man lives here would have reason to harm Charity."

I wasn't about to tell him his sister had been pregnant by somebody other than James Rainey. He'd find it out soon enough.

"Besides," he said, "she wasn't seeing anybody. Pa wouldn't let her have callers. He thought she was too young."

Overprotective, like a lot of fathers with pretty young daughters. One reason, maybe, she'd turned early wild and rebellious. I could have given Bob the names I'd come up with—Clyde Junior, Devlin Stonehouse, Jack Vanner—but I didn't do it. Charity had been too secretive about her private life to confide in her brother, and if he had any suspicions, he'd keep them to himself. This wasn't the time to open up that can of worms, either.

"It has to be Rainey, Sheriff. He must've decided not to take her away with him and Charity lit into him—she could be a hellcat when she was mad—and he ended up killing her. Dammit, when are you going after him?"

"As soon as possible," I said. "When we know anything for sure, we'll get word to you and your folks."

"That still don't satisfy."

"Then you'll just have to go back home unsatisfied."

He glowered at me, stomped over to the door, and slammed out.

Carse stirred for the first time. "More than one hellcat in the Axthelm family," he said.

"Got that right."

"He never did say how he got those banged-up knuckles."

"Better not have been from beating up on Rainey."

". . . Oh, before I forget. Telephone call for you earlier."

"Wouldn't have been from Hannah Mead, would it?"

"Nope. But you're warm."

"Uh-huh. Reba Purvis."

"Yep. Wouldn't say what she wanted."

"I know what she wants. What'd you tell her?"

"Just that you were out on business."

Maybe I'd go see her later, maybe I wouldn't. Reba's a whole lot easier to take early in the day, and that goes double when she's on the warpath. I had nothing new to tell her about the poisoning business, and I'd already found out as much as there was to know right now about Charity Axthelm's love life. Whatever else she could tell me could hold until tomorrow.

Carse untented his pulp-paper magazine, dog-eared a page, and shut it away in his desk drawer. Reluctantly, it seemed to me.

I said, "Must be real interesting, whatever you're reading."

"It is. Serial story about a character named Arsene Lupin."

"That's some handle."

"Well, he's a Frenchman, and a gentleman thief—"

"A which?"

"Gentleman thief. You know, one of those fancy-dressed nabobs, only this one steals jewels and such from other rich folks. Real clever fella, outfoxes the police and gets away with the loot."

"And he's the hero? A crook that makes the law look like fools?"

"Well, he's also a detective, sort of like that Englishman, Sherlock Holmes."

"A dandified crook who doubles as a detective. Now I heard it all."

"You ought to read one of his adventures, Sheriff. The way he works it—"

I never did find out how the French rascal works it because Bert Milbank came hurrying in just then waving a Western Union envelope. "Your return telegram from Ridgley County," he said to me. "Just came over the wire."

"About time."

I opened it up, and what it said was:

RAINEY ASSAULTED BY THIEVES STOP YES
ABLE TO TALK STOP

> T. BANNERMAN
>
> SHERIFF

Bannerman sure was parsimonious with words, whatever his reason. He'd put just enough into this wire to whet the appetite for a full explanation. Bert asked me if I wanted to reply again and I said no. No sense in wasting Peaceful Valley taxpayers' money any more than T. Bannerman was wasting Ridgley County's. All I'd get out of him was more dribs and drabs, if he was willing to dole out anything more at all.

When Bert left, I showed the wire to Carse. He said after he read it, "Assaulted by thieves. That'd seem to let out Bob Axthelm."

"Not necessarily. Sheriff Bannerman could have it wrong, a personal beating made to look like robbery. We need to know from Rainey what happened. And if it's likely he strangled the Axthelm girl and what his motive might've been if he did."

"So I'm off to Timber Point tomorrow to find out."

"First train to Missoula in the morning," I said. "Better take that magazine of yours along, Carse. Maybe that crook detective Lupin can give you some pointers on how to squeeze the truth out of a beat-up murder suspect."

THIRTEEN

A s EXPECTED, WORD of the murder got out as soon as
Clyde Rademacher started summoning the members
of the coroner's jury on Monday morning. You can't keep a
tight hitch on such a violent and suggestive crime for long,
not in a small town like Peaceful Bend that hasn't had a homicide to spice things up in more than a decade. The buzz had
already started when I left my house for the mortuary, like
the faint hum from a beehive when you give it a pass-by.
The queen bee was sure to have the news and be spreading
it far and wide. Wasn't a morsel of fresh gossip that Reba
didn't detect right off. The woman had antennae for ears.

Doc Olsen's preliminary statement to the coroner's jury
and the viewing of Charity Axthelm's remains didn't take
long once everybody was assembled. Neither did the rest of

the inquest in the town council's chambers in the courthouse, with Doc and Clyde Rademacher presiding. The only
others present beside the jurymen were me, Jeb Barrett,
Boone Hudson, and Lester Smithfield; the girl's parents and
brother weren't required to testify and hadn't come in, a
good thing because the proceedings would only have added
to their grief.

Jeb and Boone and I testified to how the body came to
be found and removed from the well. I answered the jurymen's questions as best I could, giving a watered-down account of my investigation so far. The girl's involvement with
James Rainey was known about, so I had to tell how Carse
had gone to Timber Point to question him, stressing that the
peddler was nothing more than a suspect at this point. Doc
and I had decided not to say anything about the girl being
pregnant. The fact should've been entered into the record,
but it wasn't relevant to the jury's verdict and it would only
have made tongues wag harder and impeded my inquiries.
The jury consulted for about three minutes before deliver-
ing the expected verdict of death by strangulation at the
hands of a person or persons as yet unknown.

Lester braced me before I could leave, and I had no choice
but to answer more questions from him. He wasn't satisfied
until he'd squeezed out a few more minor details that he
could print in the *Sentinel*, including a careful-worded quote
about how I wouldn't rest until the murderer was identified
and arrested.

A small crowd had gathered outside the courthouse; I
could see and hear them through the lobby window pestering

Doc and Clyde and a couple of the jurymen. I avoided being pestered, too, by going through the building to my office at the rear, with the intention of leaving that way once things quieted down. Or thought I would. Only thing wrong with that notion was that the queen bee herself was waiting there for me, buzzing mad and set to sting.

"You've been avoiding me, Lucas Monk," she said the instant I came in. "I don't take kindly to being ignored."

"Oh, now, Reba. I've been busy as the devil and I think you know the reason why."

"Of course I know . . . now. That poor foolish girl murdered by the man she was planning to run off with—"

"We don't know yet that he's guilty—"

"—but he is long gone from Peaceful Valley by now, and I'm still here and so is the woman who wants to murder *me*. But you don't seem to care about that."

"Now look here, Reba. Just because I haven't made an arrest yet doesn't mean I don't care about your welfare. I stopped by yesterday morning to see how you're getting on. Didn't Hannah tell you?"

"Yes, she told me. But you didn't bother to make another visit or even to call."

I wanted to say, *You're sore trying my patience, woman*. But I swallowed those words and said instead, "I didn't have the time. Been rushing around like a headless chicken ever since the Axthelm girl was found. There haven't been any more attempts on your life, have there?"

"Not yet," she said, purse-mouthed. "But that does not mean that creature isn't planning another. Why, she's capable of sneaking into the house in the middle of the night and murdering me in my bed."

"I doubt that. Besides, you've got that old blunderbuss of Fred's for protection."

"And I'll use it, if I have to. Don't think I won't. Just what are you doing to put an end to the witch's reign of terror?"

Reign of terror. Just like Reba to lay it on twice as thick as necessary.

"Well?" she said when I didn't answer quick enough.

"There's not much I can do right now, except try to gather more information about Grace Selkirk."

"More information." Reba sniffed. "If you mean from Hannah, you may as well look elsewhere. Her memory is as porous as a sieve."

"So she told you the Selkirk woman reminds her of someone she's seen before."

"Of course she told me. Why wouldn't she, after you quizzed her about it?"

Pried it out of poor Hannah, no doubt. I should've known that would happen. Nobody can keep a secret from Reba for long, least of all a timid woman like Hannah Mead.

I said, "If she does remember, it might be important."

"I don't see how. The witch tried to poison me because of her lust for Titus Bedford and his money."

"Maybe so. If you were the intended victim."

"What? Of course I was. You're not trying to say it was *Hannah* she was after?"

"I'm not trying to say anything. Looking at possibilities, that's all."

"Possibilities." And another sniff.

"Be doing both of us a favor, maybe, if you do what you can to help jog Hannah's memory."

"It won't do any good. I told you, her memory's porous as a sieve—even more so now, the poor thing. She still hasn't recovered from drinking that poisoned buttermilk."

I let it go. You couldn't prod Reba when she had her mind made up about something; trying only gave you a headache. I said, "I told you before I'll get to the bottom of this business, and I will. You'll just have to trust me. You can do that without hindrance, can't you?"

Sniff number three. Her mouth was still puckered. And then her brow furrowed up and she said in an exasperated way, "Must you?"

"Must I what?"

"Chew on the end of your mustache that way. It's a nasty habit. You've gnawed off so much hair on that side it looks lopsided."

I hadn't realized I was nibbling on the droop again. But I would still have done it if I had. The gnawed-off hairs irritated her almost as much as the nibbling and the mustache itself, which suited me. But lopsided? Not so far as I could see in the face that stared back at me from my shaving mirror every morning.

I chewed a little while longer, not so much to get more of her goat as a declaration of independence, before I said, "All right, then. But before you leave, I've got some questions about Charity Axthelm might be you can answer."

"What questions?"

"You told me last week that she and the peddler, Rainey, had run off together—"

"I thought then that they had."

"How'd you find out? Not from the girl?"

"Hardly."

"Who told you, then?"

"Nobody told me, at least not directly. I . . . happened to overhear her telling a friend of hers."

"What friend?"

"The one who waits tables at the Valley Hotel. Laura Peabody."

"Where'd you hear them talking?"

"In the park the day before she disappeared, last Wednesday. They had their heads together giggling about it. The girl was utterly shameless, God rest her soul."

"That why you spread the word, because she was shameless?"

Reba went up in the collar at that. "I did not spread the word, as you put it. I mentioned it to you and one or two others, that's all."

"Uh-huh. When you told me, you said you weren't surprised, that Charity Axthelm had a reputation for being a mite free with her favors."

"A *mite* free! The girl handed out her favors like penny candy."

"You know that for a fact?"

"She was less than discreet about her scandalous behavior." One more sniff. "You know the way young men talk, Lucas."

"Which young men in particular?"

"Well . . . I don't like to carry tales . . ."

"I already know the names of some of her admirers. Devlin Stonehouse, Jack Vanner."

"Yes, those two. And another whose name you'll be surprised to learn."

"Clyde Junior?"

The little gleam in Reba's eye disappeared and her forehead wrinkled up; she can't abide having somebody steal any of her gossipy thunder. "How do you know that? To whom have you been talking?"

"Never you mind how I know. Any other boys besides those three you can name?"

"Why ask me?" she said, pouty. "You seem to have plenty of sources of information."

"None as reliable as you," I said to placate her. "So. Any others you know about?"

It took her a clutch of seconds to get over her snit. Then the little eye-gleam came back. "There might be. One young scamp."

"Who would that be?"

"Tyler Fix," she said. "He was paying quite a bit of attention to the girl a while back."

"How long a while? Where?"

"Around the time of the Fourth of July picnic. Laura Peabody wasn't at all happy about it. She was sweet on him then, no doubt still is."

Well, that explained why Laura hadn't given me Tyler Fix's name when I spoke to her. "How serious was it between Charity and Tyler?" I asked.

"If you mean were they sinning together, draw your own conclusions. Or ask him, if you're of a mind to. Though I'm sure I don't know why it should matter whom she was debasing herself with. It's plain as the nose on your face who killed her, or should be."

"If Rainey's guilty, he'll pay for it."

"If? Of course he is. Just as guilty as Grace Selkirk is of poisoning my buttermilk."

Reba can wear as thin on a man as a pair of old winter long johns. I shooed her out quick before she prodded me into saying something she might make me regret. She went, but not without one more sniff. The woman sniffed as much as a snuff-taker with a bad cold.

I waited five minutes, to give her time to leave the courthouse, and then beat it out of there myself the back way.

THERE WERE TWO customers in the Fix Mercantile Company, the Eldredge sisters arguing over whether or not the bolt of cloth they were studying on was suitable for a pair of window drapes. Grover was behind the counter, squinting down from under his green eyeshade at whatever he was writing in his ledger book. I didn't see any sign of his brother.

The Eldredge sisters had heard about Charity Axthelm, naturally, being only a couple of stations below Reba when it came to back-fence talk. They threw a flurry of questions at me, all of which I deflected without letting them have anything they didn't already know. They gave up finally, unsatisfied, and went on out without making up their minds about the drapery cloth.

"What can I do for you, Sheriff?" Grover asked when I stepped up to the counter.

"Something I want to ask Tyler. He around?"

"No, he's out making a delivery. I don't know when he'll be back. Important, what you want to see him about?"

"Might be. Likely not."

"Well . . . I'll tell him you asked for him."

"No need. I'll stop back later."

Grover laid down his pencil. The set of one of his sleeve garters didn't suit him; he adjusted it. Fastidious man, Grover. "Terrible thing, the murder," he said. "Never thought I'd see the day when a thing like that would happen in Peaceful Valley."

"None of us did."

"No question that peddler did it, is there?"

"Always a question until all the facts are in."

"That button you showed me on Saturday—does it belong to him?"

"Might. Why? You remember somebody owns a coat that color?"

"No. Just wondered if that's why you were asking."

"Big part of my duties," I said, "asking questions."

When I stepped outside, a gust of ice-toothed wind bit into me and near knocked off my hat. Getting to be earflap and wool mittens time already. Tom Black Wolf had been right in his predictions so far, and I wouldn't be surprised if we had snow flurries by the weekend. Probably wouldn't be heavy enough to stick, but it'd slick the streets and roads and remind you another long winter was on its way.

I turned upstreet and was coming on Miller's Feed and Grain when Clyde Junior stepped out with a sack of oats slung over his shoulder. Sent in to fetch supplies for Karl Bruderstein, judging from the half-loaded buckboard drawn up nearby and the work clothes he wore under a heavy mackinaw. He was still working for Bruderstein, helping the farmer ready his place for winter.

He stopped when he saw me and said, "How, Mr. Monk," in that near mocking way of his. But his voice was sober enough when he added, "I just heard what happened to Charity Axthelm. A real shame."

"That it is. Whoever killed her will stretch a rope for it."

"Folks seem to think it's cut and dried who that was."

"How things seem aren't always how they are."

"So you've got doubts. That why you asked me all those questions yesterday? You figure somebody local could've done it, somebody who'd been seeing her?"

I said, careful, "Could be."

"It sure wasn't me. What I told you about us was the truth."

"There're all sorts of motives for a crime of passion."

"I never laid a hand on a woman in my life and I never will. That's gospel, whether you believe it or not."

"I say I didn't believe it?"

"But you still consider me a suspect."

"Didn't say that, either."

He shifted the sack of oats to his other shoulder. "I saw

Jack Vanner slap a saloon girl around once for spilling a drink on him. You want a likely suspect, brace him if you haven't already."

"Just what I was on my way to do."

"Luck to you, Mr. Monk. Keep your powder dry."

"I'll do that. And you keep your pecker in your pants."

To his credit, Clyde Junior didn't laugh. He tipped me a salute with his free hand and moved away to the buckboard.

FOURTEEN

JACK VANNER WASN'T hard to find. He was working with Otis Moore over on Elkhorn Street, repairing old Mrs. Wainwright's sunporch. Whacking nails into a piece of plywood siding on a side wall when I got there. Neither him nor Otis was glad to see me, Otis because he made a point of saying he was in a hurry to finish the job before the snows came.

"What you want with me, Sheriff?" Vanner said, sullen, when I got him out of Otis's hearing range. Good-looking scamp, I had to admit, even with sweat slicking his face and his mop of black hair tangled up from the wind. "I heard you plain Saturday night about leaving them Injuns alone. I ain't seen Bandelier since then."

"Pleased to hear it. But that's not why I'm here. I reckon you heard about what happened to Charity Axthelm?"

"Yeah, I heard. So?"

"You don't seem too broke up by it."

"Why should I be? I hardly knew her."

"That's not what I been told. Word is you and her were seeing each other."

"That's a goddamn lie."

"Is it?" I looked him hard in the eye. Wasn't much to see there except insolence, but he didn't match my stare for long. His gaze shifted sideways and he rubbed the sleeve of his jacket across his eyes to cover them. "Better not lie to me, Jack."

Pretty soon he said, still not looking at me square, "So what if I was seeing her? That was months ago and it wasn't for long."

"Just how long?"

"Long enough to—"

"Long enough to what? Get what you were after from her?"

"Listen, what does it matter? I didn't have nothing to do with her getting killed."

"I didn't say you did. Answer my question."

"Hell, Sheriff, she was a tramp. She liked you, she'd put out for you. She liked me for a while. That's all."

"When did you see her last?"

"Community dance two weeks ago. But we never said a word. I didn't want anything more to do with her or her with me."

"The last time you saw her in private?"

"The last time she dropped her drawers for me, you mean?"

That didn't set well at all. Neither did the insolent little sneer that went with it. I grabbed a handful of Vanner's shirt and jacket and yanked him up close. "Don't smart-ass me, boy. Somebody brutally murdered that girl. You, for all I know right now."

The sneer wiped off and his Adam's apple commenced to bob. "Hey, no, Sheriff. No. I'd never do nothing like that."

"Show some respect then."

"That peddler Rainey done it, everybody knows that—"

"Everybody don't know it. I don't know it." I shook him a little. "Now when were you last with her?"

"I don't remember exactly when. Three, four months . . . start of summer."

"Sure it wasn't five, six weeks ago?"

"No, not that recent. Three months at least, more like four."

I let go of him, gave him a little push out of my space. "Who was she seeing five weeks ago?"

"I don't know."

"No idea at all? Nobody bragging like you?"

"I ain't been bragging," Vanner said. "I'm not that kind. I got me another girl now, lives over in Riverside—"

"I asked if you heard anybody bragging."

"Uh-uh. Not in my hearing."

"Where'd you and her go to do what you done?"

"Where? Down by the river south of town."

"Not out to the old Crockett farm?"

"Place where you found her dead? Hey, no, never. Too far away. Only two times was down by the river, like I said. I swear it."

I had that rust-brown button in my pocket, and I took it out and reached it up in front of his nose. "You own a coat or jacket this color?"

He blinked at it, about half cross-eyed. No startlement in the look, though, nor any recognition. "Never did. Why?"

"Know anybody who does? Think about it."

Didn't take him long to say, "I don't recollect anybody, no."

Well, hell. Otis had quit hammering and called over to us, wanting to know how much longer I'd be keeping Vanner. No longer. I was done with him, at least for the time being.

He was an unlikable cuss, Vanner, and sure capable of lying his fool head off to cover up a crime. But he didn't have much backbone, nor much guile that I could see. Put a scare into a man like him and the truth leaks out around the edges of the lies he tells. The only leakage I could detect in his answers was his claim not to have bragged. He'd have puffed himself up to his friends first chance he had. A braggart and a bigot and a Commandment-breaker, but a murderer? Didn't seem likely, but then no man can judge another well enough to know what he's capable of under pressure, not even if he's your best friend.

WHAT WITH ONE thing and another, I didn't get to talk to Tyler Fix until late afternoon. It was after three when I went back to the mercantile, and Grover told me his brother had come back an hour or so before but was gone again. He didn't know why Tyler quit early or where he'd gone. But he'd left the store wagon out back and it was still there, so he was afoot wherever he happened to be.

I had a look in the saloons and a couple of other places and didn't turn him up. So maybe he'd headed home. The Fix place was three-quarters of a mile outside town on the northeast road, an easy enough walk. I'd have walked out there to check up if the weather had been better, but I was too tired to travel shank's mare in that cold wind. Better to shiver while seated on my hocks. Even so, I was in no frame of mind to tussle with the Model T for such a short trip, so I went back to the mercantile and borrowed the store wagon from Grover.

Elrod Fix had bought the property when he moved to Peaceful Bend and started his business thirty years ago. Grover had seen to it that the place was kept up after Elrod passed on. House and barn wore fresh coats of whitewash, and the corral gate and fence posts had a sturdy new look.

There was a big shade tree in the front yard, which would make sitting on the front porch swing tolerable in the day-time summer heat. Pretty chilly to be sitting out there on a day like this, but that was where Tyler was. He didn't move when I came clattering up in the wagon, or when I swung down and stepped up onto the porch.

What he was doing, sitting there, was brooding—the expression on his face told me that—and drinking Canadian whiskey from a two-thirds empty pint bottle. He didn't say anything by way of greeting, just looked at me and then took another swig.

I cocked a hip against the porch railing. "Little early in the day for spirits. How come?"

"My business."

"Might be mine, too, if it has to do with Charity Axthelm."

Another swallow, almost emptying the bottle, and a back-of-the-hand swipe across his mouth. "What you want with me, Sheriff?"

"I been told you were sweet on the girl. True?"

"What if it is? I'm not the one killed her."

"All right. Serious between you and her, was it?"

"My business," Tyler said again.

"The law's business, now. Serious or not?"

"Not on her part. Not after she took up with that son of a bitch Rainey."

"Before she took up with him, then?"

"Would've been, I'd had my way."

"Did you?"

"Did I what?"

"Have your way with her."

That jerked him forward, the swing swaying and creaking on its chains. "What the hell kind of question is that?"

"A sassy one, but I won't apologize for it. Well?"

"No. She wasn't that kind."

"Others say she was."

"Who? Rademacher Junior? Jack Vanner? Lying bastards."

"Never mind who. So you weren't intimate with her?"

"I told you, no."

"Never went out to the Crockett farm with her?"

"No!" He finished what was left in the bottle, looked at it, then flung it away over the railing a couple of feet to my right. Chucked it hard enough to wrench his shoulder, judging from the pain wince.

I was in a cranky enough mood as it was. "Come any closer to me with that bottle," I said, sharp, "I'd've clouded up on you."

"Go away, leave me alone," he said, sullen now, his eyes glazed and a ball of spit oozing from a corner of his mouth. "I got nothing more to say to you."

I had more to say to him, but it wouldn't have got me anywhere, the shape he was in. Frustrating as hell, trying and failing to pry something even a little incriminating out of him and the others on Charity's string. Seemed I was no closer to the truth now than when I'd started on Saturday. Little wonder I was feeling ornery.

Tyler shoved up off the swing, went stumbling into the house. I didn't try to stop him. No damn use. I climbed back onto the wagon seat, drove away from there, and abused the poor horse some, I'm ashamed to say, on the way back to town.

DAY'S END WASN'T much better than the rest of it.

No word yet from Carse, for one thing. Not that I'd expected any this soon; chances were he wouldn't get to Timber Point until late tonight or maybe not until tomorrow morning, and he'd need time to interview James Rainey. I'd told him to wire me if he learned anything important I should know right away. Earliest I could expect to hear from him was tomorrow sometime.

Sitting home didn't improve my mood, either. Old Butch was in a growly mood with an upset stomach from something he'd eaten, kept passing gas that fouled the air enough so I had to open a window. The kitchen stove half-burned my supper, the beer I intended to drink with it had gone flat, and I had a caller I could've done without seeing—Reverend Noakes, all aflutter over what he called "the vile eruption of sin and degradation in our fair community." If he had any feelings at all for the dead girl, he sure didn't communicate them to me.

And when I went to bed, I couldn't sleep. Something kept itching at the back of my mind, something to do with the murder that I'd seen or heard someplace. But I couldn't get hold of whatever it was. I told myself to quit trying to scratch what I couldn't reach, it'd crawl out of my memory on its own eventually. Good advice, but not well taken enough so I could rest my bones much before midnight.

FIFTEEN

COURT WAS SITTING on Tuesday morning and I had to testify at the trial of a half-breed named Harker I'd arrested for rustling. Wasn't much of a case—he'd pilfered and butchered one steer on account of him and his Piegan wife and brood of kids were close to starving. In the old days he'd likely have been hung without benefit of a trial, justice being damn harsh to Indian rustlers and horse thieves in particular. Now, in spite of my plea to Judge Peterson for leniency, Harker was sentenced to sixty days on the county work farm and fined fifty dollars that he'd have to work off. Justice was still harsh these days, too, seemed to me.

Turned out testifying wasn't my only court chore for the day. There was a civil proceedings matter that had to be attended to—a summons for the next court sitting that the judge wanted delivered straightaway to the defendant in a boundary dispute, nine miles out in the county to the west. Like it or not, with Carse away and my other deputies not easily reachable, I'd have to do the serving myself. Judge Peterson is even feistier than I am. When he cracks his legal whip, a man jumps or finds himself stung.

None of this helped improve my disposition. Neither did the fact that I still hadn't heard from Carse. Cranking up the flivver didn't make me any crankier, at least; she started right away for a change. And I didn't need my mackinaw or a lap robe to keep me warm this day as I rattled out of town on the northwest road. The sky was mostly clouded over, but it wasn't near as cold as it had been, the wind blowing milder with a Chinook feel. Be good to think we might be in for a last taste of Indian summer, but I wouldn't count on it. Montana weather is as changeable as a woman's mind.

I was bumping and snorting along about five miles out when I came around a turning close to where a wagon road snakes in from the wooded foothills to the west. There was a wagon on it now, drawn up unmoving a hundred yards or so from the intersection. A long squint through the windscreen let me see it clear as I neared—an old, beat-up Murphy drawn by a mismatched pair of chestnut roans. Familiar, as were the two men up on the high seat. The Hovey brothers, Lige and Wes.

What wasn't exactly familiar was what they had in the bed—a long, bulky, boxlike object roped in and covered by a tarpaulin.

They must've heard me coming and pulled up for a wait-

and-see. Pedaling down, I turned off onto the wagon road. Likely I would've done it anyhow—the Hoveys were pea-brain troublemakers—but that object in the bed clinched it. From a distance, it bore a resemblance in size and shape to Henry Bandelier's wooden Indian.

I braked the Model T at an angle in front of the wagon, blocking the road. I had my sidearm buckled on, as usual, but even if I'd been free of hardware there'd have been no cause for concern. The Hoveys were crafty rascals, but on the craven side and not dangerous. Neither Wes, who was holding the reins, nor Lige did anything but sit eyeballing me as I walked up to the wagon on the driver's side. They put me in mind of bib-overalled statues as butt-ugly as that stolen hunk of wood.

"Morning, boys," I said as I stepped up. "Long time since we set eyes on one another."

"Yes, sir, Sheriff," Lige said, "sure has been a long time." His tone said he wished it had been a whole lot longer. He was the younger of the two by a couple of years, his beard as scraggly-patched as a dog with the mange.

Wes said, "Cold as a gambler's eyeball, ain't it?" His beard had more hair in it. That, and a scar alongside his nose, was about the only way you could tell him from his brother.

"Not so much today, down here," I said.

"Sure was up to our place. Wasn't it, Lige?"

"Sure was. Cold as a witch's titty. Snow comin' any day now."

"Any day," Wes agreed.

Both of them nervous as cats and trying hard not to show it.

I said, "Now that's a curious sight."

"What is?"

"Whatever you got tied in your wagon there. Wouldn't be a wooden Indian, would it?"

"Huh?"

"The wooden Indian that was stolen last Friday night from in front of Henry Bandelier's tobacco shop in town."

Wes's eyelids flapped up and down. "No, sir, Sheriff, it sure ain't. Who'd want to steal a cigar store Indian?"

"We ain't never stole nothing in our lives," Lige said.

"Uh-huh." I took a couple of steps nearer to the bed. They turned their heads and stretched their necks to watch me. Up close, the thing tied in there didn't have a shape at all like the Cuba Libre eyesore. Which dashed the small hope I'd had that Lloyd Cooper had misidentified the thieves and Tom Black Wolf and Charley Walks Far were innocent after all. This appeared to be a big oblong box. There were holes and rips in the tarp, and through one I could see bare, weathered wood. Something else showed through another tear. I widened that one so I had a better look.

"Well, I'll be," I said, surprised. "An outhouse."

"Yes, sir, that's what she is. An outhouse, right enough."

"Can't mistake that half-moon cut in the door," Wes said.

"No, sure can't," Lige agreed.

I said, "Taking it out for an airing, are you?"

Lige laughed false. "Be a couple of jugheads if that's what we were doing, wouldn't we, Sheriff."

"Then why are you toting it?"

Wes started to answer, but Lige cut him off. "Fact is," he said, "we're takin' her over to Charley Hammond's place."

"That so? What for?"

"Well, now, we—" Wes broke off because Lige elbow-poked him in the ribs and shied him a look as if telling him to put a hitch in his lip.

"She don't set the ground right, that's how come," Wes said. "She's got warped boards and chinks in her sides. Wind comes whistling through them chinks on a cold night, it like to freeze your arse where you sit."

"Uh-huh."

"Well, old Charley's a pretty fair carpenter," Lige said, "so we figured to have him fix her up."

"He lives some ways up valley, as I recall. Seems like it would've been easier on you boys to take the outhouse to Otis Moore's shop in town."

"Sure it would. But he's gettin' on in years, Charley is, and we're askin' a favor, so we come to the idea of bringin' her to him instead."

I nodded as if I might believe him, which I didn't. Then I said, "How come you closed off the bottom end?"

"Sheriff?"

"Bottom end there. Closed it off with boards, didn't you?"

"Well, now," Lige said, and then he just sat there looking stupid. So did Wes.

"Tell you how it looks to me," I said. "Looks like you boys built yourself a big packing case out of your privy. Now why would you go and do a thing like that?"

Wes hawked and spit over the side of the wagon, away

from where I stood. "It ain't no use tryin' to fool you, Sheriff. Lige and me closed off that bottom end, right enough, but it wasn't to make a packing case. No, sir. It was something else entire we made outen that outhouse."

"Such as?"

"A coffin. We made us a coffin."

"Did you, now. Who for?"

"Old Bryce. Our hired man."

"You mean to tell me you got *him* inside there?"

"His poor remains, yes, sir. He up and died last night. Had him the ague and it turned into new-monia, and he up and died on us. Man weighed near two hundred fifty pounds, if he weighed an ounce. So there we was with a two-hundred-and-fifty-pound, six-foot-and-three-inch-high corpse and no way and no place to give him a proper Christian burial."

"How come no way and no place?"

"Well, first off, we didn't have no spare lumber to make a coffin and neither of us is handy at carpentry work besides. And we couldn't just plant him without a box."

"Uh-huh."

"Big and high as he was, why, he fit inside the outhouse just about snug. Couldn't have hammered up a better coffin from scratch if we'd tried."

"Why didn't you bury him on your property?"

"Sheriff?"

"Him and the privy both. Why bring him on down here?"

Wes didn't have an answer for that. But Lige did, such as it was. "On account of we didn't want to lose the outhouse," he said. "Had we planted 'em both, why, then we wouldn't have had one with winter comin' on. Couldn't build us a new one on account of we didn't have no lumber, like Wes said."

"Where were you fixing to bury him?"

"Sheriff?"

"Old Bryce. Where'd you intend to put him down for his final resting place? Couldn't be the town cemetery. There's a law against burying bodies there without a coffin and a permit."

His answer for that was even feebler, so feeble it brought him a kick from his brother down low on the shin where Wes thought I couldn't see. "Potter's fishing hole," he said.

"Bury a dead man in a fishing hole?"

"No, sir," Wes said, "not *in* Potter's hole, *near* it. After we bought us a plain wooden box in town. We figured a permit ain't needed for burial down there."

"That's what we figured, all right," Lige said. "Potter's hole was old Bryce's favorite fishing spot in all of Peaceful Valley. Rode on down there every chance he had."

"Uh-huh."

"Right before he croaked on us, he said as how he'd like to be buried down by Potter's fishing hole. Can't deny a man his dying wish. So me and Wes, we pulled the outhouse down and put old Bryce into her and closed off the bottom and now we're headed to town for the box and then on down to Potter's hole to find a shady spot—"

"How you figure on doing the planting?"

"Sheriff?"

"I don't see any tools in the wagon."

"Tools?"

"No pick, no shovel. Not even a hoe. Were you boys think-ing of digging a grave with your bare hands?"

"Well, shit," Wes said, disgusted, and spat out onto the road again. Only this time his aim was off. The wad smacked against the off horse's flank and caused it to frog-jump for-ward a couple of steps before he hauled it down. When that happened, the outhouse lurched and swayed and made other sounds that surprised me not a bit.

"Time you untied those ropes," I said, "and took off that canvas."

They exchanged a look. Lige said, "How come, Sheriff?"

"So I can have a look inside that outhouse."

"Ain't nothing to see except old Bryce's corpse—"

"Untie, boys. Now, and no guff."

The Hoveys were all out of arguments. They got down and began untying the ropes. Wes kicked his brother again while they were doing it, and Lige glowered at him and kicked back.

"Open up that half-moon door, Wes."

He opened it.

"Well, well," I said. "Sure don't appear to be a corpse in there to me. What would you say it's filled up with, Wes?"

He didn't have anything to say.

"Lige?"

"Well . . . I reckon it's jugs."

"Fifty or more, looks like. Packed nice and tight with bur-lap sacking all around. What's in those glass jugs, as if I didn't know?"

Lige sighed. "Corn likker."

"Uh-huh. Corn liquor you boys cooked up in that still you got hid in the hills. You and Wes and old Bryce, who's still alive and kicking and tending to his chores. That about the shape of it?"

"Yes, sir. That's about the shape of it."

Wes said, "How'd you figure we had a still?"

"There's not much goes on in Peaceful Valley I don't know about," I said.

Fact was, I'd known they were making bootleg for quite a while, just couldn't prove it. Bad bootleg, too, flavored with red pepper and chewing tobacco to give it bite and make it even more poisonous. A Piegan they'd sold some to had gotten drunk enough to cause a ruction on the reservation, and when he sobered up he told Abe Fetters where he got it and Abe told me. Carse and I had hunted for the still but never found it. I would've put the Hoveys out of the liquor business quick if we had.

"You sayin' you knowed all along we had jugs in that outhouse?"

"Had a pretty good idea once I saw that's what it was. Knew it for sure when that horse of yours frog-hopped and I heard the noises inside."

"Noises?"

"Sloshing and gurgling. Never yet heard an empty outhouse that sloshed and gurgled, nor a dead man's remains that did, either."

"Well. Shit."

"Taking the bootleg over to the reservation to sell to some of the feistier bloods and breeds, weren't you? Even though you know as well as I do it's against the law to sell firewater to Indians."

"No, sir," Lige said, "that sure wasn't what we had in mind. We was gonna sell it to the ranchers up valley near the county line. Charley Hammond, Hank Staggs . . ."

"Charley Hammond doesn't drink. He's a Hard Shell Baptist, in case you don't recollect. And Hank Staggs doesn't allow liquor of any kind on his property. And Mort Sutherland's got a bad stomach. You figure to sell more'n fifty jugs to Harvey Ames alone? Not likely. No, you were headed for the reservation, and then after you sold out, to Elkton with the money to stock up on supplies for the winter. Own up, boys. No more lies and fabrications."

Wes heaved a blowsy sigh. "All right, Sheriff, I reckon you got us. What happens now?"

"One of two things. One is I escort you and those jugs to town, dispose of the bootleg there, charge you with illegal liquor trafficking, and lock you up and keep you locked up until court sits again next week. Likely Judge Peterson'll sentence you to sixty days and order you to pay a fine."

"What's the other thing?"

I was in a better mood now, and inclined to be tolerant. "You and your brother unload the privy right here, carry those jugs to that ditch over yonder, and empty them out. Then put the jugs back inside and break them up so they can't be used again. Do that, and don't ever let me hear about you making or selling any more corn liquor, I'd be inclined to let you off with a warning."

"Every single jug?" Lige said in a kind of moan. "We spent

near three months making that batch and we're short on winter supplies—"

"Shut up, Lige," Wes said, disgusted. "You ain't got a lick of sense."

"Shut up yourself. Neither do you."

"Well, boys? What's it going to be?"

They thought it over. Took them longer than it should have because they didn't have much to think with. Then, sorrowful and resigned, they commenced to kill off every weed and stem of buffalo grass in that ditch with their godawful corn liquor.

SIXTEEN

A S SOON AS the Hoveys turned their wagon around
and headed back to the hills, I drove on to the Macy
farm to deliver the court summons in the land dispute. On
the way there and on the return trip to Peaceful Bend, my
mind kept harkening back to those two nitwits and their
hideaway cargo. That little incident made number four in the
blasted crime wave that was plaguing the valley, though this
one, at least, I'd quashed before any damage was done. And
it was the third time in less than five days that I'd had to deal
with something unpleasant hauled away in a conveyance—
Bandelier's wooden Indian, Charity Axthelm's corpse, and
the Hoveys' outhouse. All sorts of things happening in
bunches, none of them good.

But cussed coincidence wasn't all that was nagging on me.

Seemed like that outhouse and the stolen statue just might have something in common if you looked at it a certain way. Crept in on me what it was, a notion so outlandish I said, "Pshaw!" out loud and pushed it out of my head. Only it wouldn't stay pushed. I couldn't help but chew on it some more, and after a time it didn't seem quite so far-fetched as it had at first. Crazy or not, it did explain a couple of things that had been puzzling me. Trouble was, it also opened up another, even more puzzling question.

Back in town and shut of the flivver, I checked in with Mavis Cooney, who operates the telephone switchboard in the courthouse and takes messages when there's nobody in the sheriff's office. The good news was no calls and no visitors while I was away, so no further demands on my time. The bad news was still no word from Carse.

So then I went over to Main Street and H. Bandelier, Fine Tobacco and Sundries. Bandelier was behind the counter, serving nobody at the moment but himself with a Cuba Libre panatela. The look he directed at me was crabapple sour. Likewise his tone when he said, "I don't suppose you've come to tell me you recovered my Indian."

"You don't suppose right. But I'm working on it."

"You'd better be."

"Now you listen, Henry," I said, sharp. "I won't stand for any more threats, not even veiled ones. Nor any more fool notions of taking the law into your own hands. Understand?"

"Yes. All right."

"Good. Now I got a question for you about that statue. Was it carved from a solid block of wood?"

Crabapple sour to a scowly squint. "You know it was."

"No, I don't. All I know is that it's big and heavy. What I don't know is whether it's all of a solid piece or has hollow insides."

"Hollow?"

"Made from two separate carved sections, front and back, neither all that thick, fitted together and sealed and painted over. Save the Cuba Libre people money to manufacture their wooden Indians that way."

"The Cuba Libre Cigar Company is not a cheap outfit."

"Didn't say they were. Well?"

"What difference does it make?"

"Just give me an answer. Which is it?"

"I don't know," Bandelier said. "I guess it could have been made that way—I never bothered to look close or ask. I still don't see what difference it makes, hollow or solid."

"Might make some, might not."

"Well, I want it found, that's all I have to say."

"Better be all you have to say. Or do."

My next stop was going to be the high school for a talk with Miss Mary Ellen Belknap. But halfway there, that visit and my notion about the theft of the wooden Indian got put on hold.

Doc Olsen's Tin Lizzie came rattling up Main Street as I was about to turn the corner, and he pulled up and hailed me. "I was just over to Reba Purvis's house, to check on Hannah Mead," he said. "Be good as new in another day or two. Healthy constitution."

"Glad to hear it."

"She wants to see you, Lucas."

"Reba does?"

"No, Hannah. Asked me to see if I could locate you and deliver the message."

"Is Reba home?"

"No. Ladies Aid meeting."

That was a blessing. Talking to Hannah with Reba hovering around and interrupting would've been a chore. I said, "If you're not bound anywhere special, Doc, how's for a ride over there? Save me time and shoe leather."

"Climb aboard."

He dropped me in front of Reba's house. Hannah said when she answered my ring, "I was hoping it was you, Sheriff Monk. I'm glad the doctor found you so quick." She didn't need to say why. "I was about to telephone your office when he arrived and again just now."

"Remember who the Selkirk woman reminds you of?"

"Yes, I did."

We went into the parlor. Her step was stronger than it had been the last time I was here. There was color in her cheeks again, and her eyes were clear of the sickness that had clouded them on Sunday. Thinking clear again, too, evidently.

She said, "Annabelle Carter, that's who. In Denver three years ago. I didn't know her very well, hardly at all actually and not for long—just to say hello and goodbye to a few times. That's why I didn't remember right away."

"How'd you happen to know her?"

"She did some sewing for Mrs. Granger, the woman I kept house for."

"Sewing?"

"She was a seamstress. A good one. Mrs. Granger said so."

"She resembled Grace Selkirk, did she?"

"Yes, except that Annabelle had light brown hair and her skin wasn't near so pale. And she wore bright colored dresses."

"Same body type, tall and thin?"

"Not quite as thin, as I recall."

"Could they be one and the same person?"

"I've been wondering that myself," Hannah said. "Three years is a long time and I've only seen Grace Selkirk once up close. But it's possible, I guess."

"What else can you tell me about Annabelle Carter?"

"Well, she disappeared all of a sudden, not long before I left Denver and moved up here. Under a cloud, you might say."

"Cloud?"

"A man she was involved with was killed and there was talk that she had something to do with it."

"Killed how?"

"I'm not sure. It was in the newspapers, but I don't like to read about awful things like that. Or hear about them. Mrs. Granger said she didn't believe a lady like Annabelle Carter would harm anyone, not for any amount of money, and must have had some innocent reason for leaving Denver when she did."

I was on the edge of my seat now. "Oh, so money disappeared, too, did it? How much?"

"I don't remember exactly. Quite a bit, I think."

"And she was never heard of again?"

"I couldn't say if she was or not. I haven't kept in touch with Mrs. Granger or anyone else in Denver. Sheriff . . . do you really think Annabelle and Grace Selkirk could be the same person?"

"Strikes me as possible."

"But Denver is a big city. Why would she have come to a small town like Peaceful Bend and take work in a funeral parlor?"

To hide, if she was a fugitive from justice. Change of environment, along with a change in the way she looked and dressed. And a slight shift in profession from seamstress to coffin trimmer. Might be, too, if she was the predatory kind of female, why she'd gone to work for Titus Bedford. Wouldn't have been difficult for her to find out when she showed up here and spotted his ad in the *Sentinel* that Titus was wealthy and unattached. Move into his house, then make an effort to seduce him.

I didn't say any of this to Hannah, just sat nibbling on my mustache droop. Hell of a coincidence if it were true, Annabelle Carter and Hannah crossing paths in Denver and then both winding up in Peaceful Bend. But coincidences happen more often than folks might think, large and small ones both. Any law officer who has served as long as I have can vouch for that.

Hannah was talking again, saying something about the poisoned buttermilk. I said, "How's that again?"

"But even if Grace Selkirk is Annabelle Carter," she repeated, "it doesn't mean she had anything to do with putting poison in the buttermilk."

"It might. It sure might."

"I don't understand. What reason would she have?"

A good if reckless one, from her point of view. Afraid that Hannah would recognize her, which made Hannah, not Reba, the primary target. The Selkirk woman hadn't been spying on Reba, then; she'd followed Hannah to find out where she lived. Must've had a batch of cyanide all mixed up and close at hand, to be able to dose the buttermilk the following morning. Cold-blooded as hell, if that was the answer. Had Reba drunk the buttermilk and died along with Hannah, why, that would've eliminated a rival as well as a safety threat—two birds with one measure of poison.

I said, "You let me worry about that, Hannah. Did you tell Reba about Annabelle Carter?"

"No." Then, a little shame-faced, "But I did tell her I was trying to remember who Grace Selkirk reminded me of. I couldn't help it, she wormed it out of me . . ."

"Just don't let her worm out what you and me been discussing here. Don't tell her you saw me today at all. If she asks, you haven't remembered a thing."

"Oh, I won't say a word to her, Sheriff. I promise I won't."

Well, I hoped she would keep her promise, but I wouldn't have bet on it. Reba had that unholy knack for ferreting out secrets, and Hannah was weak-willed and a mite short on what the good Lord puts between a person's ears.

SEVENTEEN

THE *PEACEFUL VALLEY* Sentinel did business in a small shop on Sycamore Street, half a block from Main and the Valley Hotel. Lester Smithfield, who had more energy than a bull in heat, ran the place by himself. Wrote most of the copy for the four-sheet weekly, took and made up the advertisements, set type, cranked out the pages on his old handpress. He also did all the job printing—posters, pamphlets, business stationery, and the like—that was his main source of income. His only employees, if you could call them that, were three kids who delivered the *Sentinel* for a nickel an hour. Not that Lester was tightfisted, just frugal.

The old handpress was clattering away in the back room when I came in, Lester hard at work. I went back there to interrupt him. He took off his eyeshade, sleeved a sheen of sweat off his forehead. That forehead is like no other I've ever seen. It's got deep-cut grooves in it, crosshatched into squares you could play games of tic-tac-toe in. Grooves in his cheeks, too, only not as deep or squared. What makes this even odder is that he's not an old man, just forty or so, and the top of his head is as groove-free and shiny bald as a baby's butt.

He directed his hungry newshawk's look my way. "New developments on the murder, Lucas?" he said, eager.

"Not yet. Still waiting on word from Carse."

That puffed a little wind out of him. "You'll keep me informed?"

"Sure thing. Meanwhile, there's something else you can maybe help me with. You read big-city newspapers regular, as I recall."

"Some, yes. As often as time permits."

"Any from Denver?"

"The *Post.*"

"How's your memory?"

"Sharp as a tack, if I do say so myself."

"There was a homicide case down there about three years ago," I said. "Man killed and money stolen, and a seamstress named Annabelle Carter disappeared sudden under suspicion. Ring any bells?"

"Annabelle Carter, Denver homicide, three years ago." Lester's checkerboard forehead deepened even more when he was studying on something. Wasn't too long before he said, "I do recall that, yes. Caused a stir down there if I'm not mistaken."

"Did it?"

"A man named . . . let's see, now . . . Bowfinger? Bow-ringer? Something like that. Owned a small factory. Anna-belle Carter was his lady friend, more likely mistress."

"How'd he die?"

"I'm not sure," Lester said. "Wait, yes, I do remember. He was poisoned."

Well, now. Well! "What kind of poison?"

He did some more cogitating, then wagged his head. "That I don't recall. Why are you interested in that case, Lucas?"

"Can't tell you just yet," I said, firm. "Anything more you do recall? How much money was stolen, approximate?"

"Quite a bit. Five thousand dollars, I think it was. Miss-ing from the safe in his home—he didn't trust banks. His body wasn't found for two or three days. By then Annabelle Carter was nowhere to be found."

"Stayed that way, far as you know? Never caught up to?"

"Not to my knowledge." The grooves deepened again. "Seems to me there was more to it than that."

"How so?"

"Something about her past that came out later . . ." Les-ter snapped his fingers. "Kansas City! That's right, there was a similar case in Kansas City a few years before—man poi-soned, money stolen, sudden disappearance of his lady friend. There was speculation that Annabelle Carter might've been responsible for that crime, too, under another name."

He sounded excited now, the ink in his veins flowing hot. I was some worked up myself, but I didn't let it show. If there's one lesson all my years in law enforcement have taught me,

it's not to jump to conclusions. It sure seemed like Grace Selkirk was Annabelle Carter in disguise, and it'd be a feather
in my cap if I was to be the one to bring a lethal female pred-
ator to justice, but I had to move slow until I had more facts
and evidence.

"There happen to be a photograph of her in the *Denver
Post*?" I asked.

"No, I don't believe so."

"You wouldn't still have the issues the crime was written
up in down there, would you?" Lester was something of a
journalistic pack rat. A closet in the back room was stuffed
with old newspapers, local and out-of-town, and he had more
in his basement at home.

"I might have," he said. "I'd have to do some combing to
find out. You're after more details?"

"As many as I can get. A full description, if there is one."

"So your interest has to be pretty important," Lester said.
"You sure you can't tell me what it is? I won't print anything
you ask me not to, you have my word on that."

"Your word's always good with me. But I got to keep it to
myself for the time being. If it pans out, you'll be the first to
know and that's a promise."

"Just tell me this. Can I sow some journalistic oats with it,
if and when? And I don't mean in the *Sentinel*."

"Didn't figure you did."

"Well? Is the answer yes?"

"Might well be."

He blew out his breath with a sound like a wind whistle.
"My God," he said, "how I would dearly love a genuine scoop!

The murder of the poor Axthelm girl is the biggest thing to happen in Peaceful Valley in the dozen years I've owned the *Sentinel*, but it's more or less local news. I don't mean to sound callous, but . . . well, you know if anybody does how I feel."

That I did. Lester fancies himself a big-time journalist trapped in a small-time journalist's bailiwick. Long as I've known him he's been on the lookout for a major news story, the kind that'll get him noticed by one of the premium papers in this state or some other and lead to the sort of newspaper work he craved to be doing. I'd always figured it would never happen, that he'd be here until he died or somebody made a buyout offer for the *Sentinel* he couldn't refuse, and I reckon so did he.

I said, "If you'd hunt for those issues of the Denver paper soon as you can, I'd appreciate it."

"Right away. Might take me a while—they're likely to be in my house, if I have them at all. There's something else I can do, too. I know a reporter on the *Post*—I'll send him a wire."

"Good man, Lester. Thanks."

He responded to that with a deep-grooved grin and headed straight to his storage closet.

THERE WAS NOTHING more I could do right now about Grace Selkirk, except make sure she hadn't suddenly decided to pull up stakes. If she was the fugitive Annabelle Carter and she hadn't disappeared again since I questioned her on

Friday, chances were she intended to stay put for the time being. Keep out of Hannah Mead's way, get her hands on a pile of Titus Bedford's money, finish him off with a dose of potassium cyanide, and disappear again.

She'd gone from two big cities, Kansas City and Denver, to small-town Peaceful Bend and kept to herself while she set her sights on fresh prey. Where she'd been and what she'd been up to the past three years was anybody's guess. But she'd picked the wrong backwater to hole up in, and fate or whatever you wanted to call it had stepped in and forced her into a decision: leave without Titus's money or stay put and take bold action to get rid of the woman who might recognize her. Picking the latter was her arrogant mistake, whether she knew it yet or not. Likely she still believed she was safe enough here, even with a hick sheriff's eye on her—a hick sheriff who to her mind wasn't smart enough to figure out that Hannah Mead and not Reba Purvis had been the primary target of the buttermilk poisoning.

My excuse for stopping by the Bedford Funeral Parlor was to ask Titus if he was planning to come to the Commercial Club tomorrow night. Wednesdays is the night when the local muck-a-mucks gather to play cards, drink a little too much beer, and listen to the Hot Stove League tell lies about their adventures when they were young and full of piss and vinegar. He said he'd be there for our usual game of billiards. Grace Selkirk was there at the parlor, all right, attending to her trimming—an ironical profession, when you thought about it, for a woman who might well be guilty of filling more than one coffin.

It was on my mind that I ought to warn Titus his life might be in danger, but I didn't do it. Calculated risk. He wouldn't believe me without more than speculation and circumstantial evidence, and if it turned out I was wrong about her, I'd be opening up a snake's nest that was liable to get me bit. He ought to be safe enough until I could be certain. So I told myself, anyhow.

There was a wire from Ridgley waiting for me when I got back to the courthouse. Mavis said it'd been delivered over an hour ago. About time, I thought, and ripped open the envelope.

RAINEY NOT OUR MAN STOP BACK
TOMORROW NIGHT EIGHT PM TRAIN STOP
CARSE

Short and none too sweet. "Rainey not our man." Carse must be sure, else the wording wouldn't be so definite. Damn! I'd had my doubts about the peddler's guilt, but it would've made my job a sight easier if he had strangled the girl and been made to confess. Now it seemed we had another murderer besides Grace Selkirk in our midst. Which of the young sports I'd spoken to who'd sampled Charity Axthelm's favors was it? Or, hell, was the guilty man somebody else entirely?

I WAS SITTING in the old Morris chair in my parlor, Butch sleeping on the floor beside me and passing snores instead of gas for a change, when Lester came knocking. He had a thin fistful of newspapers that he waved like flags when I let him in.

"Two issues of the *Post*," he said. "All I could find at home. Not much in either that I didn't tell you this afternoon, I'm afraid."

"Meaning no description of Annabelle Carter?"

"Just a general one."

I squinted through the news stories in the two issues. The victim's name was Bowringer, Horace H. Bowringer, and his factory business had been the manufacture of boots and other footwear for men. His body had been found in his bedroom, dead two days from *cyanide* poisoning. By then Annabelle Carter, seamstress, reputed to be his "inamorata," was long gone without a trace. The amount of the cash missing from his safe was more than Lester had remembered, over six thousand dollars.

Annabelle Carter was described by an acquaintance of Bowringer's as "an attractive, buxom brunette of slender build, possessing a flair for colorful hats and fashionable clothing." Buxom wasn't a word I'd have used to describe Grace Selkirk, but in those loose black dresses she wore, it was difficult to tell what her shape was underneath.

"Nothing in either issue about Kansas City," I said when I was done reading.

"No, that was reported later. I ought to have the issue or issues, but I can't find one anywhere." Lester made a rueful face. "My basement is a mare's nest, much as I hate to admit it."

"Uh-huh."

"But I wired the *Post* reporter I know, Jordan Unger, asking for details about the Kansas City homicide. And for as complete a description of Annabelle Carter as exists in their files—identifying marks, habits, peculiarities other than cold-blooded murder for profit."

"Good. How soon you reckon you'll hear back?"

"Hard to say. Jordan was a friend when we both worked on the *Cheyenne Leader*, but I haven't had any contact with him in years. I marked the wire 'Urgent' and asked for a quick reply, but I suppose it depends on how busy he is. I'll let you know as soon as I hear from him, Lucas."

All I could do was hope it was soon.

WHAT WITH THE Grace Selkirk situation and Carse's statement about James Rainey to occupy my thinking, the notion I had about what happened to Henry Bandelier's wooden Indian had gone right out of my head. But it came back quick enough on Wednesday morning. My route to the courthouse took me down Main past Bandelier's tobacco store, and when I got to within viewing distance I yanked up short and stood staring.

Be damned if that butt-ugly Cuba Libre eyesore wasn't back where it used to be, on the boardwalk smack next to the shop's front door.

EIGHTEEN

"THEY BROUGHT IT back in the middle of the night," Bandelier said. He didn't sound happy about it. Anger still gleamed in his beady eyes and his mouth was pinched tight when it wasn't spewing words. "I came to open up a few minutes ago and there it was."

"Who brought it back?"

"Well, who do you think? The same two who stole it."

"Anybody see them this time?"

"How should I know? Nobody told me if so."

"Jury's still out on whether or not Tom Black Wolf and Charlie Walks Far stole it in the first place," I reminded him.

"Not as far as I'm concerned. Those two bucks are responsible, all right. For stealing it *and* for defacing it."

"Defacing?"

"Did you take a close look before you came in here, Sheriff?" Bandelier said, kind of contemptuous.

"Didn't examine it, no. Looks just the same to me."

"It's not the same. Come on, I'll show you."

I went back out on the boardwalk with him. He half-squatted next to the wooden Indian and jabbed a finger at the base back toward the rear. "There," he said. "See what those damned heathens did?"

I bent for a look. The sun was out again today, pale and frosty and playing peekaboo from behind a scud of clouds; a ray of it fell on the spot where Bandelier was pointing, so I could make out the thin slice line clear enough. The line was about eight inches long, running from the bottom of the base up one of the poorly carved legs. I knew right away what it was. Saw cut that had been filled in and painted over. Expert repair job, too. When the sun hid behind one of the clouds, you could barely see the line.

"I wouldn't call that defacing," I said. "Fixed neat like that it's hardly even vandalism."

"Oh, sure, stick up for the Flatheads like always. Dammit, they near ruined it. And for no damn reason except pure meanness."

"So you think Tom Black Wolf and Charlie Walks Far stole the statue, took it all the way out to the reservation, cut the slice in the bottom there, repaired it, and then brought it back again—all out of pure meanness. Doesn't make much sense when you look at it that way, Henry."

Bandelier sputtered some. "I don't see any other way to look at it."

I did, maybe, if the notion I'd had yesterday was right—and I was beginning to think it was, pretty close anyway. But I was not about to share it with Bandelier, now or ever.

"If it was those two," I said, "why do you suppose they brought the statue back last night?" That was the one question my notion didn't account for, though it might when I had more time to think on it. "Big risk stealing it in the first place, double the risk hauling it back and setting it up again."

"Who knows what a war-whoop will do? They don't think the way a white man does, if they think at all."

"Uh-huh."

"Probably got scared you'd finally arrest them. But I suppose you won't bother to do that now, either."

Cost me an effort, but I let the insult slide past. We'd drawn a little knot of onlookers as surprised as I'd been that the statue had come home to roost, and while Bandelier and I were talking quiet, or at least I was, some of them were within earshot. If Bandelier realized he had an audience, he'd puff up the way he had in Monahan's on Saturday night and make a loud anti-Indian, anti–Lucas Monk speech. Before that could happen, I took a grip on his elbow and steered him back inside the store.

"You got your statue back, Henry," I said then. "That ought to be enough to satisfy, the damage being as minor as it is."

"Well, it isn't enough." He started for the counter, then swung back to face me again, frowning. "All those questions you asked about my Indian yesterday, whether it was solid or hollow. You have some idea why those heathens cut into it the way they did?"

"No. I just figured it'd be easier to haul around if it was hollow."

Pretty flimsy, that spur-of-the-moment explanation, but Bandelier didn't question it. He went back behind the counter, saying sour, "I don't suppose they'll ever be punished for what they did."

"They will if I can prove them responsible. I'm not done investigating, Henry. But right now I've got more important business to attend to. Or have you forgotten what happened to the Axthelm girl?"

"I couldn't even if I wanted to, with the whole town talking about it." Then, half sulky and half snotty, "You expect to get to the bottom of that, too, someday, I suppose?"

The devil with you, Bandelier, I thought on my way out. You and that public nuisance of yours both.

THE PEACEFUL BEND High School was on a rise of ground above Municipal Park, overlooking the ball field—a redbrick building the city fathers had scratched up the funds for a dozen years back to replace the old wood frame schoolhouse. It had boosted attendance from the outlying areas, being bigger and having more classrooms. So had the hiring of two new teachers, both of them well thought of, and an expanded curriculum. Took some of the burden off Miss Mary Ellen Belknap, too, and allowed her to concentrate on her best subject, history, and on establishing the school library.

I thought I might have to wait to see her until she finished teaching a class, but she turned up alone and busy in the small room that served as both her office and the library. The door was open, so I took off my hat and stepped in without knocking, clearing my throat as I did to let her know she was about to have company.

She looked up from a stack of papers on her desk and peered at me through her spectacles. She was a little thing, Mary Ellen, not an inch over five-foot, gray-haired now but her blue eyes as bird-bright as ever. "Good morning, Sheriff Monk. What brings you visiting?"

"A small matter you can help me with. All right if I close the door for privacy?"

"As you wish."

I closed it and went to stand in front of her with my hat brim twitching around in my fingers. She was only about ten years my elder, but when I saw her in school like this, I always felt like I was fifteen again and about to be punished for truancy or pitching spitballs at girls.

"Have you found out who did that awful thing to the Axthelm child?"

"Not yet. But I'm working on it."

"I should hope so. But that can't be why you're here. I don't believe I saw Charity more than twice since she graduated, and with hardly a passing word between us."

"No, ma'am. It has to do with Tom Black Wolf."

"Yes? The theft of Mr. Bandelier's wooden Indian, I expect. I find it difficult to believe that Tom and the Walks Far boy would resort to such foolishness."

"Unless they felt they had a proper reason."

Miss Mary Ellen sighed. "Tom has always been such a

good boy," she said. "Intelligent, well-mannered, respectful of others' property. That is why I have allowed him to borrow our books from time to time since his graduation. He never abused the privilege before, but now . . . well, it seems that I may have misjudged him."

"How do you mean, he abused the privilege?" I asked.

"The last group of books he borrowed were overdue by more than a week when he finally returned them. He has never kept books past the due date before."

"When did he return them?"

"Early yesterday morning." While I was in court, probably, which is why I'd missed seeing him. "But that is not all. I'm afraid he also mutilated one of the books."

"He did what?"

"You heard me correctly, Sheriff Monk. He tore a photograph out of an expensive history book. Oh, he admitted to having done it—an accident, he said—and he carefully pasted it back in, but it is wrinkled and smudged."

"You have the book handy?"

"On the table there by the door, the large one bound in buckram."

I went and got it and looked at the title. Uh-huh. Now that notion of mine was about ninety-eight percent confirmed. And when Miss Mary Ellen told me where the damaged page was and I looked at that, the number went up a notch to ninety-nine percent.

"I'd like to borrow this myself for a while," I said. "With your permission, of course."

Delicate little lines radiated out from the corners of her

eyes and mouth. "For what purpose? Surely you don't intend to charge Tom with damaging school property as well as with theft?"

"No, ma'am."

"Then why do you wish to borrow the book? It needs to be properly repaired."

"I'll be careful with it. As careful as if it were my own."

She didn't put up any more argument. "Very well, then. I'm sure you have a good reason for wanting it—and for evading my questions."

Smart as a fox, Miss Mary Ellen. I still felt about fifteen and some chastened when I left her office with the book tucked under my arm.

THERE WAS NOTHING waiting for me at the courthouse that called for immediate attention. In my office, I sat for a little time looking through the book. Then I pulled the telephone over and had Mavis ring up Abe Fetters at the reservation store.

"Just wondering how Chief Victor is coming along, Abe."

"Guess you haven't heard," he said. "He's gone to the happy hunting grounds."

"Died, eh? When?"

"Two nights ago. The tribe gave him a big ceremonial send-off."

So now my notion stood at one hundred percent correct.

But I still couldn't make up my mind what I was going to do about it.

I propped my feet on the desk and tried to exercise my brainpower, such as it was. Which wasn't much, judging by the results. Too many things cluttering up my head. Not the wooden Indian business anymore, that was more or less settled, and besides, it had been stuffed down into third place on my list of concerns. The other two were what occupied my time.

The itch at the back of my mind started up again, but I still couldn't seem to scratch it free. I had the sense that once I did, it would go a long way toward pointing out which of Charity Axthelm's bevy of boyfriends had seeded her and then strangled her. No use trying to force my memory to cooperate. Meanwhile, about the only action I could take was to go around interrogating each of them again, and what good would that do? The questions wouldn't be any different and the guilty one would lie to me the same as he had before.

Wasn't anything I could do, either, to find out quick whether or not we had a multiple murderess in our midst. I worked up a plan of action for when there was enough proof that Grace Selkirk and Annabelle Carter were one and the same person, if they were, but until that time came all I could do was hang and rattle.

Shortly past noon I walked over to the Elite Café and ate the twenty-cent lunch, which was beef stew and biscuits today. Buttermilk biscuits, wouldn't you know, that were light as a feather but that I had trouble swallowing in spite of myself. It was a longer lunch than it should've been, not because I lingered over extra cups of coffee but because folks kept sidling up and pestering me about the murder. I guess you couldn't blame them, but all the questions and remarks and opinions shortened my temper. Hell, a man had to eat, didn't he? And if the citizens of Peaceful Valley didn't think I was doing the best I knew how to lock the strangler behind bars, let them put a new sheriff in my shoes next election. Not that I said that out loud to anybody.

Seemed like the only place I could have any peace today was my office. I told Mavis I didn't want to be disturbed by visitors or telephone calls unless it was urgent business, and locked myself inside. Three choices then: overwork my mental faculties again to no good purpose, take a long nap, or catch up on paperwork. Paperwork won out, much as I chafed at the chore of it. Clyde Rademacher is a stickler for written reports on the doings of the sheriff's office and the Lord knew there was plenty to write about these days.

Nobody interrupted my hen-scratching before I finished the last report. Not even Reba, which probably meant she was sulking over the little set-to we'd had yesterday morning. Maybe she'd finally get the message that I wasn't interested in matrimony no matter how hard she tried and go scheming to take away some other poor soul's freedom. It was a hope, anyway.

I was straightening up my desk when the only person I cared to see, Lester Smithfield, came knocking. He said when I let him in, "I just heard from Jordan Unger."

Took me a couple of seconds to recall that Jordan Unger was his reporter friend on the *Denver Post*. "What'd he have to say?"

"Long wire, collect. I hope this is as important as you made it seem—"

"What did he have to say, Lester?"

He took two yellow sheets out of his coat pocket, but just to show them to me. He didn't need to look at them, had the message memorized. "The woman in the Kansas City crime is Harriet Greenley, evidently her real name. Wanted for the cyanide poisoning of a haberdasher named Scott and the theft of nine thousand dollars. Same description as Annabelle Carter, so there doesn't seem to be much doubt that they're the same."

"Same general description, you mean? Tall, slender, attractive in a cold kind of way."

"That, a different hair color, and one other detail. Harriet Greenley was a blond and has a distinctive birthmark."

"What kind of birthmark?"

"Shaped like a butterfly, on the left side of her neck. She was proud of it in Kansas City, evidently, made no effort to hide it. She did hide it under high-collar dresses in Denver, but her victim there, the factory owner, told a friend of his that she had it."

Hid it that way here, too? It'd explain the high collars on those black dresses Grace Selkirk wore. "Anything more?" I asked.

"No. But that birthmark means something, if the look on your face is any indication."

"Might mean something."

The tic-tac-toe grooves on Lester's forehead deepened.

"Do you have an idea where the woman is now? Jordan wants to know if that's what this inquiry is all about. So do I."

"Maybe."

"That's not an answer. Dammit, Lucas, is Harriet Greenley here in the valley, masquerading under a new identity? If so, what name? And how did you get onto her?"

"Hold your water, now. I'm not a man to go off half-cocked, you know that. I told you before you'd be the first to know if and when there's a big story, and I'm a man of my word, same as you."

He made an exasperated grumbling sound in his throat. "How do you intend to be certain? Rip a high collar off your mystery woman's dress to see if she has a butterfly birthmark?"

"In a manner of speaking," I said, "that's just what I intend to do."

NINETEEN

T ITUS BEDFORD HADN'T arrived yet when I walked into the Commercial Club at seven o'clock. Most of the other muck-a-mucks were there, Clyde Rademacher and Doc Olsen and all four members of the town council among them. Doc kept his distance, but Clyde and the councilmen descended on me, yammering for news I didn't have yet and then browbeating me the way citizens will when an arrest hasn't been made quick enough to suit them. Took me near ten minutes to get shut of them and out the door. Good thing Titus still hadn't shown up by then.

Outside I paced back and forth, waiting. The boardwalk was empty now that dusk had settled and the night had turned bitter cold; I could feel the bite of the wind all the way through my heavy clothing. Be frost again tonight, ice-skim in the morning, the first snow flurries any day now.

It was five minutes or so before I saw and heard Titus coming. You couldn't mistake the high headlight beams on his Cunningham hearse, or the heavy rumble of its four-cylinder motor. Only vehicle like it between Missoula and Kalispell. Titus was so proud of it he drove it around town now and then even when it wasn't needed. Folks looked askance at the practice when he first bought the hearse, but now nobody paid much mind.

He parked a ways downstreet and I hurried to meet him. "Sorry I'm late, Lucas," he said when he stepped out, "but I—"

"No need to explain."

"Ready for billiards?"

"Can't tonight. Carse is coming in on the eight-oh-five from Missoula. Let's sit inside the vehicle where it's not so cold."

"What for?"

"Some things we have to talk over, Titus, like it or not."

"What things? What do you mean?"

Instead of answering I went around and stepped up into the front passenger seat. Wasn't anything he could do then but slide in behind the wheel again. The spot where he'd parked was beneath one of the string of electric streetlights, and the light coming through the windscreen cast his face into sharp relief when he turned toward me.

"You and me been friends a lot of years, Titus," I said, "and you know I have your best interests at heart. But I got to ask you some hard personal questions and I need straight answers. You told me the other day that Grace Selkirk offered to occupy your bed and you turned her down. But that wasn't the truth, was it."

His eyes squinched down to slits. "Now look here—"

"No, you look here. Truth is, she offered and you accepted, maybe not at first but eventually. I'm not judging you—hell, most unattached men would say yes if the time and the need were right."

"My private life is none of your business."

"Wouldn't be under most circumstances, but it is now. I'm not asking as a friend, I'm asking as an officer of the law."

"Why? Does your prying have to do with that poisoned buttermilk business she told me about?"

"Has everything to do with it," I said. "How long've you been sleeping with the woman, Titus?"

He put a hitch on his tongue. I couldn't be sure, but when he sat fidgety with his head pulled back and to one side like he was doing now, it meant that he was chafing inside. If the light had been better, I expect I'd have seen a dark flush crawl up out of his collar.

"Days, weeks?" I said.

"Damn you, Lucas. All right. Two weeks or so."

"Uh-huh. Regular?"

". . . Yes."

"She wear a high-collar nightdress in your bed?"

"For God's sake—!"

"That's not an idle question. Does she or doesn't she?"

"She . . . at first, she did. Lately, no."

"She have a birthmark on her neck?"

"Birthmark?"

"*Does* she?"

"Yes."

"Shaped some like a butterfly?"

"Yes. Christ! What does a birthmark matter?"

"Matters a whole hell of a lot," I said, grim. "So does money. You keep much cash in the house or the funeral parlor?"

"Some, not much."

"She been after you to draw a large amount out of your bank account for one reason or another?"

Titus quit fidgeting and drew himself up stiff and tight-mouthed. "I'm not going to answer any more of your impudent questions until you tell me what this is all about."

This wasn't the right time or place, but I had to make sure the woman wasn't planning a sudden run-out. I said, "All right. But first, tell me this. Are you in love with her?"

"What? No. No!"

"Good. That makes it easier on both of us." I sucked in a breath. "I got good cause to believe her real name's Harriet Greenley, not Grace Selkirk, and she's a fugitive from justice, wanted in Kansas City and Denver for murder and grand larceny," I said, and went on to fill in the bare bones of her crimes.

He didn't want to believe it. At first he kept shaking his head, wobbly, like it was about to come loose from the stem of his neck. Then he quit that and clutched on to the steering wheel with both gloved hands, saying, "My God, my God," in a stricken voice.

I didn't say anything, just sat quiet and waited for him to

get a grip on himself. Took another minute or so before he managed it.

"It was loneliness made me weaken," he said then, low and hangdog bitter. "She looks and acts cold to others, but with me she . . . she was warm, in and out of bed, and acted like she cared about me . . ."

Sure, she did. That was how she got her hooks into a man. Play up to him, pleasure him, and then when the time was ripe to get her mitts on his ready cash, feed him a dose of potassium cyanide. Same principle as a black widow spider after the mating ritual was done with.

Titus blew out his breath in a vapor-plumed sigh. "What do you want me to do, Lucas?"

"Nothing tonight, except act natural with her. Don't give her any cause for suspicion."

"You're not going to arrest her right away?"

"Not unless she's fixing to run off again, which isn't likely if you're sure no large amount of cash is handy to her."

"I'm sure. There's not more than fifty dollars in the house and mortuary combined."

"All right. Tomorrow, then. Meet me in Judge Peterson's office at the courthouse when he opens up for business at ten."

Titus said he'd be there. I didn't need to tell him the reason; smart as he is, he already knew.

THE 8:05 FROM Missoula was seven minutes late, which by railroad standards is considered on time. I left the stove-warmth inside the depot and stepped out onto the platform when the locomotive came chuffing and rattling into the yards. Only three passengers got off, Carse the last of them toting a Gladstone bag.

He stood stretching his beanpole frame. "Riding on a train always seems to pinch up my back," he said when I joined him. "Seats are just plain uncomfortable, no matter what the railroad claims."

"Uh-huh."

"Not that driving over rough roads did my back much good, either, never mind that a Hupmobile's got better shock absorbers than a Model T."

"Rented one in Missoula, did you?"

"Had to. No train service to Ridgley County until a spur line gets built next year, just sixty-some miles of bad road." His long face shaped into a grimace. "Rental sure wasn't cheap. I hope Mr. Gilardy won't refuse reimbursement when I hand in my chit."

Morton Gilardy was the tightfisted county treasurer. "He won't," I said. "I'll see to that."

We walked down off the platform and over to Main Street, setting a brisk pace. "Have your supper on the train?" I asked on the way.

"Sandwich," Carse said. "But I could sure use something to warm me up on a cold night like this. Not coffee—bourbon-and-ditch."

"Makes two of us. But not in one of the saloons." I'd had enough prying and prodding from the citizenry for one day. "I'll buy you one at my house where we can talk in private."

When we were seated in front of the stove in my sitting

room, drinks in hand, we got down to it. I said, "What has you convinced Rainey isn't the one strangled Charity Axthelm?"

"Well, neither motive nor much of an opportunity. And he was surprised as hell when I told him she was dead, same when I said she'd been with child. Not faking it either time, I'd stake a bet on that."

"Why do you say no motive?"

"He wasn't running off with the girl. He pulled out of here the day *before* they were supposed to rendezvous."

"Did he, now. How come? Cold feet?"

Carse shook his head. "Stringing her along so he could get as much as he wanted from her. Slick-talking bugger, not worth the powder to blow him to hell, but not the violent sort."

"Then how'd he get injured so bad?"

"Couple of toughs beat him up outside Timber Point, busted his jaw and his leg and a couple of ribs. Ransacked his wagon, stole some money and a bunch of other stuff. He didn't put up much of a fight."

"Could've made that story up, couldn't he?"

"Nope. Sheriff Bannerman knows who they are from Rainey's description and has a warrant out for them. Besides which, there was a witness—a kid taking a shortcut home near where it happened. He ran for the sheriff soon as the toughs rode off."

"So that lets out Bob Axthelm. He must've got those bruised knuckles in a mix-up with somebody in Kalispell." I took a pull on my bourbon-and-ditch. I'm not much of a drinking man usually, but when there's a strain on me I'm as needful of a nerve-calmer as the next man. "Can Rainey prove he left here when he says he did?"

"Seems so. He stopped over in Hayfork that night and talked a saloon girl into going to his wagon with him. Told me her name."

"Might be she's willing to lie for him."

"Might," Carse admitted, "if she knew him from before. But I think he was telling it straight. Anyway, we can talk to her if needs be. She's still in Hayfork, and he's not going anywhere as busted up as he is."

"When did he last see the Axthelm girl?"

"Day before he pulled out, two days before she was killed. Got together then to make plans for when they'd be leaving together—her plans, not his."

"Where were they supposed to meet for the departure?"

"Down at the river, where he was camped. Said that was where they always met."

"He never went out to the Crockett property with her?"

"Swore he never heard of the Crockett property. Didn't seem to be lying about that, either."

"He have any idea who might have killed her?"

"No. She never said anything to him about trouble with another man, or about another man period." Carse's back was still bothering him. He shifted position in his chair, his long legs stretched out in front of him. "With Rainey out of the picture, I guess somebody local must've done it."

"Sure seems that way."

"You got any idea yet who?"

"I wish I did," I said. "I questioned Jack Vanner and Tyler Fix while you were away, but I didn't get any more out of them than I did out of Clyde Junior or Devlin Stonehouse."

"Tyler Fix, eh? So the girl had four lovers, not just three."

"Maybe. Reba Purvis put me onto Tyler as one of Charity's swains. He claims he never had relations with her, but he's pretty broken up about her death—drinking heavy when I talked to him."

"How you figure to find out which one is guilty?"

"That's the question. You got any suggestions?"

"None direct," Carse said. "But I been thinking, and there's one thing that don't add up just right. How come the Crockett farm?"

"How come she was killed there, you mean?"

"And how come she and whoever knocked her up picked it for their love nest? Plenty of places closer to town that're just as private. Over along the river where she and Rainey met, for one."

"That's the way I see it, too. Can't be because the Crockett place is closer to the Axthelm ranch so she could get home quick afterward, or closer to where any of the four suspects live."

"Fifth suspect you haven't found out about yet?"

"Christ above, let's hope not. This case is complicated enough, and I got too much worrying my mind as it is."

"Something else happen while I was away?"

"Plenty. Too dang much, one thing after another."

I told him about the Hoveys and their load of bootleg liquor, and about Bandelier's wooden Indian turning up back where it came from and my notion of the why and wherefore of the theft. Saving the big news for last.

He didn't scoff at the notion, but I could tell he was dubious. All he said was, "If that don't beat all. Sure is a puzzle and a caution, the way Indians behave sometimes. You going to do what Bandelier wants and arrest those two bucks?"

"I haven't come to a decision on that yet. More important things to deal with first. Whoever strangled Charity Axthelm's not the only murderer we got in Peaceful Bend, Carse. There's one even worse been hiding here right under our noses."

He straightened up in his chair. "Who?"

"The woman who calls herself Grace Selkirk. Her real name is Greenley, Harriet Greenley, and she's wanted in Kansas City and Denver. Poisoned a man in each city for their money and disappeared without a trace."

"Poison!"

"Same kind as in the buttermilk. Potassium cyanide."

"Lordy," he said, big-eyed. "But why'd she try to poison Reba Purvis?"

I said, "Wasn't Reba she was after, not directly, it was Hannah Mead," and went on to tell him why.

"Lordy," he said again. "But if you know who she is, how come you haven't arrested her yet?"

"I just found out for sure tonight . . . pretty much for sure. The more evidence we can lay hands on, the stronger the case against her. We'll be going after some in the morning."

"Take her into custody whether we find it or not?"

"Have to. Before she gets a sniff that we're onto her and flies the coop again."

Carse shook his head, the wonderment kind of shaking. Then he said, "If you wouldn't mind, Lucas, I believe I could stand another bourbon-and-ditch."

Me, too. I built us two more, light on the ditchwater.

TWENTY

FOUR OF US met in Judge Ephraim Peterson's office on Thursday morning—me, Carse, Titus, and Clyde Senior. Clyde was there in his capacity as county attorney; I'd called him from home last night to tell him what was going on.

The judge was a crusty, stiff-necked old gavel-banger. He'd been on the bench for more years than I'd been sheriff, not all of them in Peaceful Valley. He owned a home in town, but only spent about two days a week here; the rest of the time he lived with his daughter and son-in-law and a passel of grandkids in Kalispell. He didn't socialize much, so I hardly knew him except in an official capacity. Which was all right with me. His idea of justice didn't always match mine and we'd locked horns several times, often enough when an Indian was involved. He was harder on them than he was on white men, his Tuesday decision in the half-breed Harker case being the latest example, though he claimed to have no prejudice.

In the judge's favor, he was honest and a stickler for law and order. I'd fretted a bit to Clyde that he might balk at issuing a search-and-seizure warrant and an arrest warrant, either or both for lack of sufficient cause, but Clyde assured me he wouldn't and he didn't. He listened steely-eyed and scowling to what I had to say about Harriet Greenley alias Grace Selkirk and what we hoped to find in her possession. When I told of the attempt on Hannah Mead's life, he muttered, "Deplorable!" and his scowl got even more ferocious. He asked Titus if he had any objection to a search of his premises, and when Titus shook his head and said no, the judge made out and signed both warrants and handed them over without argument or cautioning. But as the rest of us were leaving he said to me, waspish as usual, "I won't stand for murderers loose in my jurisdiction, Sheriff Monk. See that you catch the farm girl's slayer, too, and don't be tardy doing it."

Out in the hallway, Clyde said to notify him as soon as we had the fugitive in custody and I said I would. Then Carse and Titus and I drove straight from the courthouse to Anaconda Street in the flivver. Titus had passed a sleepless night—dark eye-baggage told me that—but he seemed to've regained his equilibrium and had his emotions under control. He hadn't said much in the judge's office and didn't now, speaking only when asked something direct and then mostly in monosyllables. I'd had a brief confab with him before we went in to see Judge Peterson and he was certain Greenley/Selkirk had no suspicion that we were onto her. She'd wanted to share his bed again, but didn't question him when he put her off. This morning he'd told her he had a financial matter to attend to and that she should watch over the undertaking parlor in his absence.

The way his house was situated, you couldn't see the main entrance from anywhere inside the mortuary behind, so Carse parked right in front. The woman's bedroom was on the second floor, at the other end of the hall from his. She kept the door locked, but Titus had an extra key that he hadn't told her about. After he used it, I told him to wait in the hall while Carse and I searched the room.

It was tidy enough, clothes and high-button shoes all tucked away inside a chiffonier along with a leather suitcase, nothing left out in plain sight except a jewelry box and a few women's toiletry items on a glass-topped dresser. I looked through the jewelry box first. Seed-pearl necklace, rhinestone brooch, and three or four other gewgaws, none of which struck me as being particularly valuable. The chiffonier came next, while Carse poked around inside a big sewing basket and button box. The suitcase was empty and the lining hadn't been tampered with. Most of her clothing was plain black with lace trimming—no snazzy outfits, no furs or frippery. If she still owned the fancy outfits she'd worn in K.C. and Denver, she'd hid them away somewhere for safekeeping.

Then we inspected the dresser and nightstand drawers, and the seams on the brocade cushions on the only chair.

Unmade the bed and hoisted up the mattress, and Carse got down on all fours and squinted under the bed. After that we hunted for hidey-holes in the floor, walls, ceiling and didn't find any.

Nothing of criminal consequence anywhere.

But then my eye caught again on the handful of little jars and bottles atop the dresser. Might as well take a closer look, which I did. Lotions, violet sachet, face powder, black hair dye. Seduction tools, the lotions and sachet, but face powder? The times I'd seen her up close, her cheeks were pale and scrubbed clean, free of cosmetics.

I unscrewed the top from the jar. Contents looked like tannish face powder, all right; smelled like it, too. I stuck a finger down inside under the puff, wiggled it around. Ah. Something else in there at the bottom, something that had a slick crinkly feel.

I emptied puff and powder onto the glass, fished it out—a little folded packet wrapped in that newfangled stuff called cellophane. Slow and careful now, I opened the packet. More powder, white. I sniffed it, then wet the tip of my finger and sniffed that.

Bitter almonds. Potassium cyanide.

"Right there all along, more or less in plain sight," Carse said. He'd stepped up to watch over my shoulder. "Like in 'The Purloined Letter.'"

"The what?"

"Story by Edgar Allan Poe. Tells that the best place to hide something you don't want found is right out in plain sight."

"You get that out of *Adventure*, too?"

"Pulp-paper magazines aren't all I read."

Titus was there, too, now; he'd heard us talking and stepped inside. He said, grim, "So she did keep her poison here."

"Close to hand," I said. "Her weapon of choice."

"My God."

I refolded the packet of cyanide, put it into an evidence envelope I'd brought with me. "Well, now we got all the proof we need. Time to put Harriet Greenley under lock and key where she belongs."

MAKING THE ARREST should've been easy as pie, but it wasn't.

Goes to show you can't take anything for granted when you're dealing with criminals, women same as men.

There was a brick path that led from the rear of the house to the rear of the mortuary. Titus led the way along it. He'd insisted on coming along and I figured he was entitled. We went in through the empty embalming room, the formaldehyde smell strong enough in there to clog my sinuses. A low whirring noise coming from one of the other rooms told where she was.

"Sewing room," Titus said. "This way."

The sewing room was off a short hallway, the door open so the bell could be heard if anybody came in the front way. Harriet Greenley was seated in front of a pedal-operated machine, stitching two pieces of pillowcase satin together for a medium-size casket on a roller table nearby. She had her back to the door so she didn't see or hear us come in until she let up on the pedal. Must've sensed she had company then, more company than just Titus, because she sat stone-still for a few seconds before slow-turning her head.

I reckon she could tell from our expressions that this wasn't any ordinary visit, that Carse and I were there on a mission. But she didn't show it. Looked steady at us, not a flicker of emotion in her ice-blue eyes.

"Yes?" Just that one word, flat.

I said, "Stand up, Miss Greenley."

A tiny flicker, nothing more. "What did you call me?"

"Greenley. Harriet Greenley."

"You're mistaken. My name is Grace Selkirk."

"There's no use pretending any longer," Titus said. "Sheriff Monk knows who you really are."

I said to him, "You keep still and let me do the talking." Then to her, "It's my duty to take you into custody—I have a warrant for your arrest. Do as you were told and stand up."

"On what charge?"

"Charges, plural. Unlawful flight to avoid prosecution for murder and grand theft in Kansas City and the same in Denver. The attempted murder of Hannah Mead right here in Peaceful Bend."

"That is preposterous. I am not Harriet Greenley and I did not attempt to murder anyone."

"I got proof that you did."

"What proof?"

"The cyanide you had hid in your jar of face powder."

I thought that would crack her, but it didn't. She had more nerve and gall than H. Plummer, the Virginia City outlaw leader. She didn't say anything, just sat there like something that'd just been dug up from inside a snowdrift.

"Do as you're told, Miss Greenley," I said, sharp, "and stand up. You're under arrest. Carse, put handcuffs on her."

She stayed put. I thought I'd have to go lift her up myself and I sidled a step toward her, and that was when she moved. Fast, faster than I'd ever seen any woman move. She dipped a hand into the pocket of her dress and came up out of her chair, all in the same blur of motion. What she yanked out of that pocket caught me and Carse both flat-footed, our jaws hanging open.

A double-action Remington derringer.

Thumb-cocked and aimed straight at my gullet.

"Stand where you are," she snapped. "One more step and I'll shoot you dead."

I could've kicked myself. You go to arrest a woman whose weapon of choice is poison, you don't expect her to have a Henry D. hidden on her person. Fact that she did and that I was looking square into the muzzle made me mad. One thing I can't abide is having a firearm pulled on me.

"Put that peashooter up," I snapped back.

"You're not taking me to jail, you goddamn hick sheriff."

Hick sheriff. That made me even madder. "Put it up, I said. You're not about to shoot me or anybody else."

"You think not? Come ahead, then."

Carse, on my left, murmured, "Go easy," out of the side

of his mouth. I didn't move, didn't turn my head so much as a fraction. My eyes were on that derringer.

She said, "First thing I want you to do is disarm yourself. Take your revolver out of its holster with your left hand, put it down slow on the floor, and kick it over to me."

I had my coat open enough so she could see the Colt's handle poking up. But not open wide enough so I could make a pass at pulling it. I'm no quick-draw artist anyway, and even if I could get it out and up before she ventilated me, I wasn't sure I'd be able to squeeze the trigger. I'd never shot anybody in my entire twenty-five years in law enforcement, though I'd come close on a couple of occasions. Having to put a bullet in a woman, bad as this one was and despite the situation, was a sickening prospect.

"No."

"What did you say?"

"You heard me. I'm not about to let you have a second pistol."

"I can take it off your dead body."

"You'd have to empty both barrels to put me down. Do that and my deputy here will be all over you before you can get away."

Temporary standoff. Her eyes were narrowed to slits and her face all clouded up under the white pallor, like rock showing under a skim of glare ice. Maybe a minute crawled off, the silence crackling the way it does during an electrical storm.

"Titus!"

The name came out of her sudden, in a half shout. It jerked him out of his lumpish standstill, set him to shuffling his feet.

"Give me your keys."

"Keys?"

"You always carry them with you. Take them out, drop them on the floor."

He hesitated, but when she waggled the derringer at him, he did as he'd been told. Didn't need to drop the key ring; he was so fumble-fingered it slipped loose of his grasp as soon as he had it out.

"Now kick them over to me."

He obeyed again. Plain enough what she wanted them for. The thought of her trying to make a getaway behind the wheel of his Cunningham hearse was ludicrous as hell, but that was what she was fixing to do. And God help anybody who got in her way. The woman wasn't just a cold-blooded poisoner, she was damn sure crazy. And about as dangerous as they come.

I couldn't let her get away clear, maybe harm somebody else. As soon as she bent at the knees and started to reach for the key ring with her free hand, I took action. Didn't think about it, just sucked in my belly and jumped at her in a side-ways dodge.

Things got pretty confused the next few seconds. The der-ringer bucked and cracked loud, and a .30-caliber rim-fire bullet slashed air past my head. Carse yelled something and there was another noise that I found out afterward was him shoving Titus out of the line of fire. And I slammed into Harriet Greenley with my upraised shoulder before she could shoot again, sending her arse upwards across the sewing machine chair.

She hit the floor with a thump, screeching. I managed to stay on my feet with the help of the table, threw myself down on her as she struggled to get up, and yanked the derringer out of her fingers. Carse was there to help me by then, and a good thing because it took the two of us to roll her over, hold her down, and handcuff her. She kept screeching the whole time, using profanity the like of which would've impressed a drunken muleskinner. Carse and I were both sweating and panting and marked with scratches by the time we finished the chore.

Now I knew what it was like to rassle with a wildcat. And to come within a few inches of being shot. Little wonder I was sweating and shaky. I sure as hell hoped this was the first and last time I'd have either experience.

TWENTY-ONE

W E HAD TO hog-tie Harriet Greenley to keep her from kicking, stuff a wad of satin cloth in her mouth to shut her up. Even then, she thrashed around and made furious throat noises and threw looks of hate my way that would have melted a snowman.

I sent Carse to fetch the flivver. Titus had recovered his equilibrium, but he still looked a touch green around the gills. Hell, I probably did, too.

"You took an awful chance, Lucas," he said, half admiring and half chastising, "rushing her the way you did."

"Think I don't know it? But I couldn't let her get away. No telling what she might've gone and done."

"You could have been killed."

"But I wasn't. That's all that counts."

When Carse came back, we hauled the woman out to the Model T and laid her in the rear seat. I should've had Titus do my part of the carrying instead, but I didn't think of it until my bursitis started giving me hell on the way. I sat back there with her to keep her from squirming around too much. Wasn't any way we could get her to the courthouse and then into the county lockup without being spotted. It wouldn't take long before word got out and put the whole town into an uproar.

Getting the woman into a cell didn't take any effort, but removing the rope and handcuffs did. Once her legs were free, she fetched a kick at Carse's privates he saw coming and dodged away from just in time. Then he shoved her flat on her face on the cot and sat on her legs while I unlocked the cuffs. We got out of there quick before she could do any more than lash us with another hail of profanity. The click of my key in the lock was the sweet sound of relief.

I locked the evidence packet of cyanide and the Henry D. in the safe, then telephoned Clyde Senior to let him know we had Harriet Greenley in a cell, not mentioning the trouble we'd had getting her there. He said he'd take care of notifying the police captain in charge of the murder investigation in Denver—the officer's name had been in the issue of the *Denver Post* Lester showed me—and have her removed from our custody as soon as the necessary legal arrangements could be taken care of. He felt as I did that the sooner we were shut of her, the better. Likely there'd be a jurisdictional squabble between Denver and Kansas City over which would get to try her first, and there wasn't any use in

Peaceful Valley getting into it whether Judge Peterson agreed or not. When it comes to court trials in cases like this, even an attempted double poisoning takes back seat to cold-blooded homicide for profit.

I left Carse in charge and beat it down to the *Sentinel* office to keep my promise to Lester before he got wind of the arrest from somebody else. From his excited reaction, you'd have thought I'd brought him news of a big cash windfall. Well, in a way that's what it was—a windfall, I mean, the exclusive story he'd been panting after his whole life. He pressed me for details, and I gave him enough to satisfy for the time being. One thing I didn't tell him was how I'd jumped into the muzzle of that derringer and nearly got my fool head blown off. He'd worm that out of Carse or Titus soon enough, and likely make me out in print to be some sort of hero. I wouldn't mind the feather he'd put in my hat for catching a wanted murderess, but there wasn't much heroic about the way I'd done it. If I had to do it over again, I was embarrassed to think that I wouldn't.

Lester rushed off to the jail to see what he could get out of Harriet Greenley, and I headed over to Tamarack Street. I didn't relish the idea of dealing with Reba just now, but she had the right to know the full story and Hannah even more so. Better they should hear it from me, officially, before the rumors and the gossip started flying.

I should've known Reba would already have the news. She got it from Ellie Rademacher, who was sitting with her in the parlor when Hannah showed me in, the two of them sipping tea from china cups and chattering together like magpies. Right away they transferred their attention to me, all hungry-eyed and eager for the bits and pieces Ellie hadn't been told on the telephone by Clyde Senior. Not so much like magpies, then. More like a pair of bone-picking carrion birds.

"Clyde said you were nearly killed, Lucas," Ellie said. "My Lord, it must be awful to have had such a close call."

"It wasn't all that close."

Reba said, "Don't be immodest. You're lucky to be alive. And if those scratches are any indication, that crazy woman fought you tooth and nail. The bloody one on the side of your neck there wants treating with antiseptic before it festers. Hannah, fetch the iodoform from the upstairs bathroom."

Hannah, who had been hovering nearby, started out. I stopped her by saying, "No need. I'll take care of it later." I resisted removing a glove and exploring the neck scratch. It couldn't have been too bad since I hadn't noticed it paining, and neither Carse nor Titus had mentioned it. Reba making mountains out of molehills again.

She sniffed. "You're always putting things off, Lucas Monk. Such as informing me that the woman not only tried to poison me, she's a multiple murderess and thief wanted in two other states."

"I didn't know it for sure until this morning."

"But you suspected it. Why didn't you tell me?"

"Wasn't any point."

"No point? She might have tried to murder me again while you were dawdling around looking for proof."

"I wouldn't have let that happen. And it wasn't you she aimed to poison, it was Hannah." I explained why, not that Reba didn't already know that, too. "That's why I came here now, to give you the straight of it."

"*After* she was put in jail. After the fact."

She had the damnedest knack for getting under a man's skin. I said, "I don't have time to argue, Reba. I'll be going now."

I swung around and headed out. She called something I didn't listen to, and when I kept on going without answering, she hopped up and followed me into the front hallway. I got the door open, stepped out onto the porch. But before I could close it behind me, she said, sharp and smug, "I *told* you she was an evil witch, didn't I?" and closed it herself.

That was Reba for you. Always had to have the last word, and often as not it was an I-told-you-so.

I EXPECTED HARRIET Greenley to still be yelling and cussing when I got back to my office, but there wasn't a peep from the cellblock. Lester was still there, occupying my desk chair and talking to Carse.

"She wouldn't speak to me, wouldn't even look at me," he said to me. "I couldn't get a blessed word out of her."

"Went mute all a sudden," Carse said. "Just lays on her bunk and stares up at the ceiling."

I thought but didn't say, Thank God for small favors.

Lester transferred his tail from my chair to a corner of

my desk. He was still in high spirits despite being denied an interview by the prisoner, for he'd inveigled Carse to blab about what had taken place at the undertaking parlor. He started badgering me to tell my side of it, why I'd done what I had, and I had to oblige him. I downplayed my actions as much as I could, leaving out the part about feeling like a damned fool afterward and still, but when I finished he winked at me and said he'd write it up as "fearlessness in the face of death."

Fearlessness in the face of death. Uh-huh. Well, that kind of praise would stand me in good stead with the citizens of Peaceful Valley—for a while, anyway. The next election was a long way off and voters have short memories for accomplished deeds and long memories for unaccomplished ones. If I failed to solve the murder of Charity Axthelm, that was what they'd remember when they cast their ballots.

Carse and I were busy as hell after Lester went haring off to interview Titus at the mortuary. First we had to arrange for temporary partitions to be put up in Harriet Greenley's cell to give her necessary privacy, then I had to go and talk Boone's wife, Francine, into agreeing to act as matron. And all the while one or both of us had to fend off visits from city and county officials. The only ones we didn't fend off were Ed Flanders, my night deputy who came to find out firsthand what all the commotion was about, and Clyde Senior when he showed to report that he'd been in touch by wire with the Denver police.

"How long before they send someone up to take her off our hands?" I asked him. "Tomorrow?"

"Probably not that soon," Clyde said. "More likely first of next week."

Damn. All we could do was hope Harriet Greenley stayed clammed up until then.

I TOOK MYSELF out of commission and went home around four o'clock. Long, hard day and I figured I was entitled. The way the weather was shaping up, it'd be the kind of night to sit quiet in front of a hot fire and lick my wounds in private. The wind had turned blustery, with plenty of teeth in it, the sky was loaded with black-bottomed clouds, and the temperature had already plunged into the 20s. No snow yet, but it wouldn't be long now.

I took Buster for a walk, fed him, then carried in half a dozen armloads of lodgepole and tamarack logs from the woodshed and stacked them in the cabinet next to the fireplace. My teeth were chattering by the time I finished that chore. I laid a fire and got it burning, brewed myself a cup of coffee, sat down in my chair with my shoes off to toast my cold feet. But I was too restless to sit still—leftover nerve-frazzling from the morning's adventure.

I got my toolbox and attended to some repair work I'd been putting off. Put a new washer in the leaky kitchen faucet, hammered a piece of tin over a mousehole on the back porch, went down into the basement and fixed the loose latch on the ground-level window. When I was done with that, my eye caught on the jars of fruit and pickled vegetables Tess had put up the last year before she took sick. Clingstone peaches had been her specialty and there was one quart jar left. I hadn't been hungry until then, but just looking at those peaches made my mouth water. I took the jar upstairs and pig-ate everything including the juice.

Full dark by then, the only sounds the wind, the crackling fire, and Buster's snoring. I'd left word with Ed Flanders, and with Mavis to pass on to the night switchboard operator, that I wasn't to be disturbed except in a dire emergency. So far, so good. If anybody did come calling, it had better be on urgent business or I wouldn't even open the door.

With my stomach full I wasn't quite so restless anymore. I picked a book out of the glass case in the parlor, occupied my chair again with Buster on the rug alongside. I'm not the reader Carse is, or that Tess was—she'd built up a nice little home library by mail order—but I like a good story now and then when I'm in the mood. Reading a book helps me unwind, too.

This one put me to sleep in the middle of a story called "The Girl and the Graft," no fault of Mr. O. Henry. The wind woke me up, howling and yammering at the doors and windows. I must've been out for a while because the fire had banked and the room felt chilly again. The clock on the mantel gave the time as 9:45.

Hell with it. I went to bed.

Buster ambled in after me, and as soon as I climbed into bed in my long johns he whined to come up. I let him do it. Poor old dog has creaky joints and not much meat left on his bones, and it'd be cruel to deny him comfort and warmth once the weather turns wintry.

"Settle down now," I said to him. "And if you want to stay up here tonight, you better not start farting again."

He gave me his aim-to-please look, yawned, curled up. And farted, loud.

I sighed. But I didn't have the heart to push him off the bed. I turned off the lamp and buried my nose in the pillow, and for a change I had no trouble dropping into a deep sleep.

Not long before dawn I dreamed that I was having another wrestling match with Harriet Greenley, or maybe the same one as in the mortuary, and that she had the whole right side of my body pinned down so that I couldn't struggle free no matter how hard I tried. The trapped sensation woke me up. And when I was shed of the dream, I realized that I *was* being pinned down—by Buster, who'd crawled up next to me for body heat and was stretched out snoring on my right arm. He'd been laying there so long the arm was numb from shoulder to fingertips.

I sat up muttering, shoved him off the bed, and commenced to rub circulation back into the dead limb. Pretty soon my fingers began to tingle and I could move it again. I kept on rubbing.

And while I was doing that, that memory itch started up again. Only this time it was more than just an itch—it was what I'd been trying to remember.

All of a sudden I wasn't groggy anymore. Funny how a man's mind works. Free it from worry-clutter, and it kind of refocuses itself while you sleep and lets you see things plain that you couldn't see before. Not just the one memory and what it might mean, but others, too, now and how all of them tied together.

What I was studying on wasn't ironclad proof of who'd strangled Charity Axthelm, not yet. But it wouldn't take long, by God, to find out whether or not I was right.

TWENTY-TWO

THE TEMPERATURE WAS down to 15 degrees and it was snowing when I left the house in the morning, bundled up in my winter clothes and hat with the rabbit fur earmuffs. The snowfall was light and not sticking, but judging by the look of the cloud swells overhead, the flurries would keep coming. Just what I needed to make what lay ahead even more of a task.

I found Doc Olsen seated in one of the mahogany booths at the Elite Café, pouring catsup over a trio of runny fried eggs. He has his share of bad habits, Doc, but none worse than that. If you're hungry, watching him swirl his fork through the red and yellow mess will make you lose your appetite. If you're not hungry, watching him slurp it up will keep you that way for a spell.

"You know what that looks like, don't you?" I said as I slid in across from him.

He glowered at me. "Sure I know, I'm a doctor. I happen to like my eggs this way. So sue me."

"Grouchy this morning."

"You'd be grouchy, too, if you'd spent half the night with Emma Lou Hansen's bowels."

Doc started eating and I busied myself beckoning for a cup of coffee and then looking elsewhere until his plate was more or less clean. Then I said, "You remember when I came to see you about the poisoned buttermilk—"

He cut me off before I could get any more said. "Poisoned buttermilk! I had to hear the news from Emma Lou, a bed-ridden old lady, that Grace Selkirk was guilty of it and a wanted fugitive besides."

"Harriet Greenley. That's her true name."

His glower got even darker. "Why didn't you confide in me?"

That was pretty much the same thing Reba had said to me yesterday. Hell's bells, I couldn't go around taking every-body into my confidence on such a ticklish matter, could I? I said to mollify him, "I'm sorry, Doc, I should have told you. Just so damn much on my plate these days."

He didn't say anything to that, just wiped his mouth with his napkin. But he did quit glowering.

"The day I came to your office," I said, "you were treating Tyler Fix for some ailment. What was it?"

"What's that got to do with anything?"

"I don't know yet that it does. Well?"

"Allergy rash. From an accidental fall into some buck-brush."

"Where was the rash?"

"His right shoulder and forearm. One of the scratches was deep and threatening to fester."

"Could the scratches have come from something other than buckbrush? Blackberry thorns, say?"

"Could've, yes," Doc said. "Hard to tell exactly what causes that kind of wound or what a person's allergic to. What're you getting at, Lucas?"

There wasn't anybody within earshot, but I lowered my voice anyway. "You recall what was growing close to the well where we found the Axthelm girl's body?"

"Blackberry tangles . . . Good Christ. Tyler Fix?"

"Shh. I don't know yet. Maybe. The man who carried her out there blundered into the tangle before he dropped her in—the blackberry thorns caught in her coat prove that."

"You better have more evidence than a few thorns and a rash on his arm. Even if it was blackberry that caused the rash, they're common as weeds."

"I know it." I got out of the booth and up on my feet. "Thanks, Doc."

"You going to hold out on me again?"

"For now. You'll be the first to know if and when there's anything important to tell."

"Hah. I'll believe that if and when it happens."

Back outside, I walked fast upstreet to Fix Mercantile. Grover was behind the counter, waiting on a customer who was buying a pair of wool mittens and grousing about how winter seemed to be coming earlier every year. Tyler wasn't anywhere to be seen.

My presence seemed to make Grover uneasy; he kept glancing at me while he finished the transaction. When the customer left and I went up to the counter, he pasted on a thin smile that went away as soon as I spoke.

"I don't see your brother," I said. "He out on a delivery?"

"No. He stayed home this morning. He . . . he's not feeling well."

"Hung over, is he?"

"Why would you think that?"

"He was drinking pretty heavy when I saw him the other day. Grieving for Charity Axthelm, seemed like at the time."

"He has no cause to grieve for her . . ."

"Don't tell me you didn't know he was seeing her on the sly."

Grover wagged his head, but not as if he was denying it. He quit looking me in the eye.

I said, "You recollect me showing you the rust-brown button off a man's coat? When I asked if you recalled selling a coat that color, you hesitated before saying you didn't. How come?"

"I . . . don't recall hesitating. Why would I?"

"Only one reason I can think of."

"I never sold a coat like that, Sheriff, I swear I didn't."

"Never sold one, but you had one in here once and Tyler took a fancy to it and you let him have it. That's right, isn't it?"

"No . . ."

"Grover," I said, sharp, "I'm all through listening to lies

and evasions. I want the truth now. Did you let Tyler have a coat that color?"

"Where . . . where'd you find the torn-off button?"

"I think maybe you know the answer to that. One more time: Did you give your brother such a coat?"

He drew a breath, said to a point past my right ear, "All right. Yes. More than a year ago."

"You ask him why he lied when I showed the button?"

"Yes, but he said it wasn't the same color and his coat had all its buttons. That was all he'd say."

"And you took him at his word."

Grover said, lame, "We're not close, we don't talk much." Meaning he hadn't wanted to know any different.

"Tyler still have the coat?"

"I . . . don't know. He doesn't wear it very often if he does."

"Saved it for special occasions, likely, such as rendezvous with Charity Axthelm."

"For God's sake, you don't think that Tyler—"

"I'm heading out to your farm now to have another talk with him. You know what's good for you, you won't try to get there ahead of me and warn him."

"I won't. But you must be wrong, no matter how it looks. He . . . my brother would never . . . never . . ."

Wasn't anything more I could or needed to say. I turned my back on Grover's misery, went out, and set off on another fast walk, this one to the courthouse to collect Carse.

"Come on," I said, "we're taking a ride in the flivver and you drive better in this weather than I do."

"Where we going?"

"To make another arrest. Charity Axthelm's murderer, this time."

THE CUSSED MODEL T decided to be balky again. Carse spent near ten minutes cranking before he could get spark enough to keep the motor running. As short as the distance was to the Fix farm, the heater wasn't likely to put out enough warm air to stave off the chill so we had to use the lap robes. And even with the side curtains buttoned up tight, the wind found ways to come whistling in.

The sky was still full of white flurries when Carse took us out of the barn and on through town. The thick, low-hanging overcast had darkened the day enough so that he had to put on the headlamps. And to drive slow on account of patches of ice and the snow starting to stick now. I had trouble seeing clear through the swirling flakes and the rime forming on the windscreen, but it didn't seem to bother him. He'd been comfortable handling the flivver from his first time at the controls after the county bought it. Didn't matter what the weather or the road conditions were, he just plain liked to drive.

Neither of us said anything as we headed out the north road. Would've been hard to talk over the engine rumble and exhaust farts. Anyhow, I'd already given him a fast rundown, on our way to the garage, of all the things that'd put me on to Tyler Fix.

The boy's visit to Doc Olsen and the skin ointment he'd

left with was the first—that nagging memory itch. Then there was the way Tyler flinched when he threw the empty whiskey bottle off his porch, as if his arm was paining him. And the blackberry thorns stuck in the girl's dress. And his claim not to know anything about the rust-brown coat and torn-off button. And the fact that he was the most likely to've taken Charity Axthelm to the abandoned Crockett property, having passed it any number of times whilst out making his deliveries. And the heavy drinking that'd started after the body was found—too heavy to've been caused by grief over a girl he claimed not to know well.

Guilt was the reason. And fear. He'd put her body down the well with the idea that it'd soon be hidden by the winter snows, that it might not be discovered until the Crockett farm was finally sold and by then it'd be a skeleton and he'd be long gone from Peaceful Valley. When Jeb Barrett's boys found it by accident after only three days, it must've thrown him into a panic. He didn't dare pull up stakes right away; would've amounted to an admission of guilt if he had. All he could do was wait, and drink, and sweat, and hang on to the false hope that I wasn't smart enough to catch him.

The only thing still in doubt was the homicide motive. Pretty safe assumption that he'd strangled Charity Axthelm in a fit of rage, but what had set him off? Her planning to run away with James Rainey? The revelation that she was pregnant, if she'd even known it yet herself? Some other trigger? Well, I'd know soon enough.

The Fix place loomed ahead. Carse turned in, rattled us into the farmyard. No lights showed inside the house, at least none you could see from out where we were. The house and the outbuildings had a deserted look under their splotchy dusting of white.

Carse yanked on the brake and shut off the headlamps, but left the motor running. We climbed out. Nothing moved anywhere except the stinging snow, and there were no sounds other than the wind and the flivver's engine. If Tyler was inside, he'd sure have heard us coming. And just as sure, there'd be a rifle or two and maybe a handgun in the house. I hadn't drawn my weapon when we walked in on Harriet Greenley yesterday, a mistake I wasn't about to repeat again. Just no telling what a desperate criminal will do, drunk or sober— that was a lesson learned and learned well. I opened my mackinaw, worked off my right-hand glove, then transferred the Colt from holster to coat pocket. I kept my hand in there on the handle so my fingers wouldn't numb. Carse did the same with his sidearm. He doesn't usually go armed, but I'd insisted this time.

We eased up onto the porch. From there I could hear a steady clattering somewhere at the rear—sounded like a loose screen door banging in the wind. Front door wasn't locked; the knob turned under my hand. I motioned Carse to stand aside, then stood aside myself and reached out to shove the door open. Nothing happened. I let a few seconds slide away before I gestured to him and we entered, cautious.

The front room was empty. We moved slow through the rest of the house. Tyler wasn't anywhere to be found. In what I took to be his bedroom—near-empty whiskey bottle on the nightstand—the bedclothes were half off the mattress and wadded up on the floor. I opened the wardrobe for a quick look inside. No rust-brown coat. Even if he hadn't noticed the missing button, he'd have gotten rid of it sure with the shoulder and sleeve ripped open by the blackberry tangles.

The house was icebox cold. Grover must've lighted the kitchen stove before he left, but the fire had gone out long since. The reason was that the back door stood wide open, and each flap of the screen door blew chill air and swirls of snowflakes inside.

Carse said, "Looks like Tyler flew the coop in a hurry."

"If he did, it was by wagon or on horseback."

"Have to be bad spooked to do either in weather like this."

"We'll have a look out back."

We went outside, shutting both doors after us. The stubbled grass in back showed what might've been man tracks here and there, but it was hard to tell on account of the sifting of snow. Head down into the wind, boots crunching on thin skins of ice, I led the way past the well and the wire-fenced chicken run. At the barn I tugged one door half open, peered into the hay-and-manure-spiced gloom. First thing I saw was the shape of what figured to be the only other conveyance on the farm besides the mercantile wagon, an unharnessed buckboard.

Carse said when he saw it, "Guess that leaves horseback."

"Seems like."

I widened the door gap enough for us to pass through. And once I was inside, with the moan of the wind muffled some at my back, I heard what sounded like a nicker. When my eyes adjusted, I spotted a lantern hanging from a hook to one side of the door; I took it down, fumbled around in my pants pocket for the matches I carry, found and used one to light the lantern. Held it up high so the flickery glow chased away shadows and let me see all the way back.

Horse in one of the stalls, all right, a ewe-necked dun. The other stalls were empty.

"You recollect how many horses the Fixes own?" I asked Carse.

"Can't say I ever knew."

"I don't believe more'n two." And Grover had hitched one to the store wagon for the ride into town this morning. "But we best have a look in the tack room, see if there's a saddle missing."

The tack room was a cubicle next to the rear doors. We tramped down the runway to it, the dun nickering again and shuffling around in his stall, looking to be fed, as we passed by. The door was open a few inches, and when I stepped up close I made out a faint sound inside, a funny kind of slow, rhythmic creaking. I pushed the door all the way inward with my left hand, holding the lantern up with my right.

"Jesus, Mary, and Joseph!"

That was Carse, coming up next to me. What we stood looking at in there froze my voice box, brought the taste of bile into my mouth.

Tyler Fix, hanging from a rope looped over a thick cross-beam.

Wind drafts coming through chinks in the wallboards made the body move, the rope creak. The boy's face was the color of spoiled liver, eyes popped and tongue showing at a mouth corner, but that wasn't all there was to see. Pinned to the nightshirt he wore was a piece of writing paper with a loose smear of words scrawled on it.

I killed Charity Axthelm.

TWENTY-THREE

I MOVED FIRST, inside for a closer look at the body. Carse followed and I handed him the lantern, then worked off one of my gloves and felt a dangling wrist with two fingers. Not hunting for a pulse, wasn't any use in that, but to test the body temperature.

"He don't appear to be stiff," Carse observed.

"Cold and still limp. Dead no more than a few hours."

"Must've come out right after his brother left for town. Fixed the rope, climbed up on that little stool over there, and jumped off."

"Looks that way."

"Couldn't live with his guilt, so he saved the county the expense of a trial and did the hangman's job himself. Lordy."

I didn't say anything. I felt bad about this, real bad,

because I could have prevented it. Would have, if it hadn't taken me so damn long to put the finger on Tyler.

"Cut him down now?" Carse asked.

"No. I want Doc Olsen to have a look first."

"Don't seem right to just leave the kid hanging there."

"He wouldn't be any deader or more pitiful laid out on the ground."

I gloved my hand again, took the lantern back, and lifted it up as high as I could reach. All Tyler's shell had on it was the nightshirt, a half-buttoned pair of jeans, and scuffed boots. The note on his shirtfront was fastened on with a safety pin. Close up, the four smeared words appeared to have been written with a piece of charcoal—likely a cold ember from a fireplace or stove. Looked to be some kind of contusion on the side of his neck, but in the flickery lantern light I couldn't tell just what it was. Rope burn, maybe.

Wasn't much to see in the room except for the short three-legged stool Carse had mentioned. It lay upended against the inner wall a distance from the body, one of the legs loose and crooked. Nothing else in there—two worn saddles, saddle blankets, bridles, hackamores, another harness, some tools on a bench—appeared to've been disturbed.

"All right," I said, "let's move out."

Carse hesitated. "I can stay here and keep watch while you drive in and fetch Doc."

"No need for either of us to freeze our asses here and the house is just as cold. Tyler's not going anywhere. And you know you handle the flivver better than I do when it's snowing."

We left the barn—the dun horse had to be fed, but that could be tended to later—and tramped out to the Model T. Carse said as we climbed in, "We going to tell Grover about his brother right away?"

"Not until after Doc examines the body."

We rode back to town in silence, the snowfall now just a light, steady sifting of flakes. I sat with my feet braced against the floorboards, hanging on to the strap and gnawing on my mustache. Seemed to take longer than it had coming out to travel the three-quarters of a mile, maybe because I wasn't paying attention to the road.

Carse stayed in the flivver while I went upstairs to Doc Olsen's office. Doc was in, fortunately, saving us the trouble of having to go hunting for him. He took one look at me and said, "You look all het up, Lucas. Bad for your blood pressure."

"Good reason. You wanted to be the first to know if anything happened, you got your wish. Tyler Fix is dead."

Nothing much ruffles the old bird. One thick eyebrow hoisted, his only reaction. "The hell you say. Don't tell me you had to shoot him?"

"Hell, no. Found him hanging in the tack room out at the Fix farm. Note pinned to his shirt saying he killed Charity Axthelm."

"So. Suicide."

"Appears to be. Get your bag, Doc. Carse is waiting downstairs in the flivver."

He didn't waste any time. Couple of minutes later the three of us were headed back out to the north road, and ten minutes after that we were in the Fix barn. I relighted the lantern we'd used before, and a second one I'd spotted on a bench on the way out earlier so we'd have plenty of light. Then we crowded into the tack room.

Doc peered up at the corpse. "Never a pretty sight," he said, sour.

"You seen many other hanged men?" I asked him.

"A couple, and I don't care to see any more after this one. Go ahead and cut him down."

I fetched the three-legged stool. The loose leg made it wobbly, but it held my weight when I stepped up and sliced through the rope with my Barlow knife. Carse had hold of the body, lowered it and stretched it out. Tyler had soiled himself when he died; the odor hadn't been too bad before, cold and drafty as it was, but with him laid down it was stronger. The dun horse had stamped around and let loose with a couple of mournful whinnies when we passed by his stall, and he started in again now. I told Carse to go fork some fresh hay for the animal. No use in all three of us being in the tack room with the body and the smell.

While Doc was doing his examining, I cut the hang rope off the stanchion it was knotted around and pulled it down slow and easy. Ran an ungloved hand along the section that had been curled around the beam.

"Hard to tell in this weather how long he's been dead," Doc said, straightening up. "Rigor mortis hasn't set in yet. Three to four hours, at a guess."

"That was mine, too."

"His neck's not broken. Strangled, from the look of his face."

"Uh-huh." I unpinned the note from the nightshirt, folded it careful, and tucked it into my coat pocket. Then I bent to squint at the contusion I'd noticed earlier. "What do you think caused that?"

"Hard to tell. Light's too poor."

"Blow of some kind, fist or hard object?"

"Could be. Why?"

"That stool there," I said, pointing. "You saw where it was lying before, over by the wall—a good seven feet from where he was hanging. Could he have kicked it over that far in his death struggles?"

"Must have."

"Doesn't strike me as likely. One stool leg's loose. Kicked hard, I'd say. Hard and angry."

Doc conjured up one of his scowls. "What're you getting at?"

"Take a look at the rope, the fibers where it was looped around the crossbeam."

Carse came back just then. He picked up the rope, looked at it first, then held it out for Doc's inspection. "Rubbed up, not down," he said.

"The wrong direction. Tyler didn't climb up on the stool and jump off, he was strung up and the stool kicked away afterwards."

Doc said, "Good Christ, Lucas. You're saying he was murdered."

"Afraid so. Hauled out of his bed, slugged, carried out here, and hanged. I don't like it any more than you do, but the evidence doesn't lie."

"But the suicide note—"

"Anybody could've written it, the way it's scrawled."

"Anybody who? I thought you were convinced Tyler killed the Axthelm girl."

"Still am," I said. "It's possible somebody else did it, murdered Tyler and framed him to throw off suspicion. Then again, framing doesn't have to be the motive."

"No? What the devil is, then?"

"I don't know yet. But I'll find out."

He wagged his head. "*Another* murder. My God, that's the last thing we need right now."

The last thing, yes—another murder. And now not just four crimes in this goddamn epidemic, but five.

Five!

I HAD CARSE drop me at the mercantile, take Doc to the Bedford Funeral Parlor, tell Titus to come pick up Grover on his way to the Fix farm, and then come back to fetch me. Doc could ride out to the farm with Titus to collect Tyler's body, if he was of a mind to.

Main Street was mostly deserted and there wasn't anybody in the mercantile except Grover, listlessly stocking the canned food shelves. He came hurrying over as soon as he saw me walk in.

"Did you see Tyler? What did he say?"

"I saw him and he didn't have anything to say. Afraid I got some bad news for you, Grover. Your brother's dead."

"Dead? Tyler's dead? You didn't—?"

"No."

"Then how? What happened?"

"Close up shop and get your coat. Then I'll tell you."

He put a CLOSED sign in the door, locked it, and turned off the lights. When he came back buttoning into his coat, I laid it out for him, terse. Tyler'd been a boy, Grover was a man. He took it with just a couple of flinches.

"I guess I can understand how Tyler could've lost control and murdered that poor girl," he said, "but to go and hang himself? That's even harder for me to believe."

"He didn't hang himself. Somebody strung him up."

Another flinch. "Who'd do a thing like that? Why?"

"Don't know yet. You have any ideas?"

"No. My God, no."

I took the false suicide note from my pocket, unfolded it. "Recognize the handwriting?"

"No."

"Couldn't be Tyler's, done in a hurry?"

"No. Everything he wrote was back-slanted. Where'd you get this?"

"It was pinned to his nightshirt."

"Damn whoever did this. Damn him!"

"Was Tyler home last night?"

"No. He came in late, drunk. I don't know where he'd been."

"Talk to him then?"

"I heard him stagger in, that's all."

"Anybody come around looking for him last night or this morning?"

"No."

"Where was he when you left the farm?"

"In his bed. Sleeping."

"Sure he was asleep?"

"I tried to wake him up, but he called me a dirty name, shoved me away, and started snoring again. That's the last thing he said to me, that dirty name. His final farewell." Trace of bitterness in the way Grover said that last.

He turned to look out past the drawn window shade. "You said Titus Bedford was coming. What's keeping him?"

"Hasn't been that long. He'll be here pretty soon."

Carse rumbled up in the flivver first, the Cunningham hearse two or three minutes later. Grover unlocked the door as soon as he heard it, relocked it after we stepped out onto the boardwalk. Just Titus in the hearse; Doc must've decided to stay in town. Grover got in with them and I waved Titus on before depositing myself in the flivver.

"Where to?" Carse said. "Garage?"

"How much gas left in this rattletrap?"

He checked the gauge. "Half a tankful."

"More than enough. No need to stop at the garage."

"Where, then?"

"Tyler Fix was no lightweight," I said. "Took a strong man with good balance to carry him into the barn, then hang him from that beam. The way I see it, the motive has to be vengeance—an eye for an eye, a neck for a neck. Only three men could've found out it was Tyler strangled the girl. Grover's one, but he's not powerful enough or filled with enough rage and hate. The other two are named Axthelm. And J.T.'s got that bad leg from the war."

"Which leaves Bob."

"Which leaves Bob. Young, strong, hotheaded Bob Axthelm."

TWENTY-FOUR

I T HAD STOPPED snowing by the time we reached the Axthelm farm. The thin frosting on the ground was already
melting off. Tree branches, fence posts, power poles and lines
were still decorated in white, but unless we had another
freeze tonight the last of it would be gone by morning.

The jouncing and sputtering noises the Model T made
brought J. T. Axthelm and his wife out into the farmyard as
they had before, both from the house this time. The woman
stayed on the porch while he hobbled down to the foot of
the steps. There was no sign of Bob. Just the same, I unbut-
toned my coat and pulled the skirt back over the Colt's handle
before I opened the passenger door and stepped out.

Carse got out, too, and came around to my side. I motioned him to stay put there, went ahead to where Axthelm

stood. Same stoic look on the weather-brown face as on our last visit. Occurred to me for the first time that he might have Indian blood. Well, so what if he did? His wife wasn't anywhere near as good at hiding her feelings. There was worry in her careworn face, tension in the tight clasp of her hands on the collars of a sheepskin draped over her thin shoulders.

I asked, "Your son around, Mr. Axthelm?"

"No. Off the property." Same flat monotone as before.

"Expect him back soon?"

"Don't know when he'll be back."

"That the truth? That he's gone off somewhere?"

"I don't lie."

Mrs. Axthelm said, a tremor in her voice, "Why do you want him? What's he done?"

"We don't know that he's done anything. Just want to talk to him."

"What about?"

"Has to do with Tyler Fix."

"Oh, God! I told J.T. there'd be trouble. I told him!"

Axthelm said, sharp now and without looking at her, "Hush up, Miriam."

I said, "Why did you think there'd be trouble, ma'am?"

"The letters."

"Hush!"

She didn't listen to him. What showed in her face now was fear and she was caught in its grip. "I was going through Charity's things last night, and there they were. I still can't believe—"

Axthelm whirled on her. "Damn you, woman, those letters are private family business!"

"Not if Bob's gone and done something crazy. He—"

From the way he stomped his good foot onto the lower
riser, I thought he was about to go up the stairs after her. I
laid a hard hand on his arm. "Leave her be and let her talk,
Mr. Axthelm."

He glared at me, tried to shake loose. I held on, match-
ing his glare. It wasn't much of a standoff. I had the authority and his wife had already let the cat out of the bag. Not a
contest he could win and he knew it. He said, "Shit," and the
tension went out of him. When he took his foot off the step,
I released my hold on him.

"The letters you found, Mrs. Axthelm," I said then. "Written to your daughter by Tyler Fix?"

"Yes. Three. Long, rambling . . ."

"Saying what?"

"How much he . . . he loved her. Full of all sorts of intimate . . . Oh, my Lord, I thought at first they must be lies
but she wouldn't have kept the letters if they were. I never
thought Charity was that sort of girl. Never! Never!"

"Sweet young virgin," Axthelm said, and let loose with a
glob of spit. "Whore's more like it."

"No, J.T., please don't say that—"

"True, ain't it. And with child to boot."

I said, "The letters mentioned that, her being with child?"

"No," Mrs. Axthelm said. "Just that he . . . he wanted her
to be pregnant, wanted to marry her. And that she'd best be

true to him, he couldn't stand the thought of her with another man."

"Threatening, then?"

"Only the last one. After she took up with that man Rainey."

"Son of a bitch is the one who killed her," Axthelm said. "Not Rainey, Tyler Fix."

I said, "You're right, he is. Why didn't you bring those letters to me soon as you found them?"

"We couldn't," she said. "Bob took them."

"When?"

"Last evening. He heard me crying in Charity's room. He came in and took them away from me, read them. He . . . he was furious. He ran out and saddled his horse and rode off. J.T. couldn't stop him."

"Take anything with him? Clothes, weapons?"

She shook her head, but Axthelm said, "Rifle in his saddle scabbard."

"You haven't seen him since?"

"No," she said. "I've been worried sick."

"Went after Tyler Fix, didn't he?" Axthelm said. "Hurt him bad?"

I had to say it. "Tyler Fix is dead."

A thin wailing sound came from Miriam Axthelm. She leaned heavy against the porch railing.

"Bob killed him?" Axthelm said. Then, when I nodded, "Wasting your time here then. He won't be coming back."

"If he does, advise him to give himself up."

"So he can hang? Not damn likely."

Wasn't anything more for us here, Axthelm was right about that. I felt bad for him, for her. But there wasn't anything I could do for them. I turned away, started back to the flivver. Behind me I heard Mrs. Axthelm say in a moaning voice, "Both our children, gone. Nothing left now, nothing but emptiness and sorrow . . ."

I got into the flivver and Carse drove us out of there. We were passing through the ranch gate when a thought came to me so sudden I spoke it out loud.

"Where did he spend the night?"

Carse said, "How's that again?"

"Bob didn't find Tyler alone until this morning. Where'd he spend the night?"

"Watching the Fix house, waiting his chance."

"No," I said. "Bitter cold last night. He's no fool, he wouldn't chance frostbite staying outside. Had to've sought shelter, for him and his horse both, and not on the Fix property where he might be spotted. Dawn or later before he went there."

Carse chewed on that. "Not too many places he could've gone."

"I can think of one he'd be drawn to."

"Where?"

"The place where his sister died."

THE BARREN, SNOW-SPRINKLED Crockett farmland looked even more forlorn under the leaden, low-hanging clouds. As if it hadn't just been abandoned by people, but by God, too. Carse braked near the entrance to the lane. You couldn't see the farmhouse and outbuildings from there, with the rise between them and the road.

"Drive or walk in?" he asked.

I'd given that some thought on the way. "Drive. Long walk in the cold, and we'd be out in the open, exposed. He's got a rifle, remember. If he's there, no telling what his frame of mind is."

"He'll hear us coming if he is."

"Be keeping watch anyway. More protection for us here in the flivver."

Carse took the brake off, pedaled into low gear, and set us bumping along the overgrown lane. When we cleared the top of the rise, I sat forward to peer through the crusty windshield. Forlorn wasn't the right word for those falling-down buildings and the twisted remains of the orchard. Dead fitted better—rotting gray carcasses with their bones showing.

Carse must've had the same feeling. "Spending a night out here'd be like spending one in a graveyard," he said.

"You wouldn't mind if you had nowhere else to go and you were hell-bent on revenge. Just the place to work yourself into a killing rage."

"By listening to ghosts? Gives me chills just thinking about it."

Down into the farmyard, slow. Nothing moved anywhere except the wind, stronger than it had been earlier. The front door of the house was shut, but the boards that'd been nailed across it were hanging loose; a board had been pulled off one of the windows, too, so that part of a broken pane of glass was visible behind it. The wind could've been responsible, as it likely was for the tattered muslin curtain stirring inside the window, but I didn't think so.

"Pull up over to the left," I told Carse, "where you can get a better look at the stable and corral. And leave the motor running."

He did that, set the brake again. Opened his door and stretched his long frame out and up, to look over the top of the door.

"See anything?"

It was a clutch of seconds before he said, "Movement in the stable, just a glimpse. Might be a horse in there."

I got out on my side, but not until I'd ungloved my hand and switched the Colt sidearm from holster to mackinaw pocket. Nothing happened then, or when I took a couple of slow steps toward the porch. Two more paces and then I stopped, waited a few seconds, then cupped my hands around my mouth and shouted loud.

"Bob! Bob Axthelm!"

The only answering voice belonged to the wind.

I yelled his name a second time, then a third.

Behind me Carse called out, "Horse back there for sure."

That settled it. Time to take the bull by the horns. "We know you're in there, Bob!" I shouted. "Come on out!"

Silence from the house.

"Come on now. We're not leaving until you show yourself."

Silence. But then, as I was about to try again, he finally

acknowledged. "What you want with me, Sheriff?" Standing close next to the busted window, I judged. Rifle in hand? I sure hoped not.

"Talk."

"About what?"

"Come on out and I'll tell you."

"How'd you know to come here?"

"Didn't. Just a guess when we didn't find you at home."

Silence. No movement at the window that I could make out, not even the curtain stirring now, and the door stayed shut.

"You coming out?"

Silence.

"Don't be stubborn, Bob. Hurts a man's throat, shouting this way with a wall between us. Let's talk like men, face-to-face."

". . . I asked you what about."

"Tyler Fix."

Silence. Then, "He's the one murdered my sister, not the peddler." Those words came in a rush. Hard to tell with the wind blowing, but I thought his voice sounded heavy with strain. Still with some of that killing fury in him? His conscience bothering him, too, maybe.

"We know that, Bob. He hanged himself this morning, suicide note pinned to his shirt confessing."

"Justice, by Christ."

"That's right. You coming out now?"

No, not yet. Thinking it over in there, something I didn't want him to do.

Then, "Hanged himself, you say, confessed. Then why'd you come looking for me?"

"To tell you about it, ease your mind."

"Bullshit. You could've let Pa tell me."

"Step out, and we'll hash it over."

"You know I done it. That's it, isn't it? You know about those letters, you know I killed him."

"Bob . . ."

"I had a right. Son of a bitch got Charity pregnant, tried to talk her into marrying him when she told him. She laughed in his face, he said. Wanted the peddler, not him. That's why he went crazy and strangled her."

"All right," I said. "Now listen to me. Lay your rifle aside, if you got it in there with you, and walk on out here. Slow and easy, with your hands up where I can see them."

"No! You're not taking me to jail."

The muscles all along my back were tight as bowstrings. I took a firmer grip on the Colt's handle. "It won't go too hard for you. Judge and jury'll understand why you did it—"

"I won't go to jail!"

"Bob, it's your only choice—"

"Like hell it is!"

Three or four tense seconds. And then the muffled crack of a rifle shot.

I threw myself down flat, jamming my jaw into the half-frozen ground. Pure reflex. So was dragging the Colt out of my pocket. For when I raised my head, I didn't see a rifle barrel protruding from the busted window and realized that the shot hadn't been directed at me, or at Carse over by the flivver yelling. It'd been confined inside the house.

I scrambled to my feet, the bursitis in my hip hurting fierce as I ran up onto the porch. Bob hadn't barricaded the door; it whipped inward when I slammed my shoulder against it, staggering me as I burst through.

He was on the floor over by the window, a long-barreled Winchester lever-action beside him, blood all over one side of his face. Not dead—twitching and moaning with his eyes rolled up. I took a couple of deep breaths to settle my nerves, slow my pulse rate. Carse came running in as I waved away powder smoke, bent for a closer look at Bob Axthelm. The blood was oozing from a black-edged furrow that extended from jawline to hairline.

"Damn fool's lucky to be alive," I said. "Only thing saved him is how hard it is to shoot yourself with a rifle. Must've stuck the muzzle under his chin and it slipped sideways when he pulled trigger."

"Wound doesn't look too bad," Carse said.

"Bad enough, but he'll live."

We carried him out to the flivver. The blanket his sister and Tyler Fix had used for their trysts was still in the trunk box where we'd put it on Saturday; we wrapped his head in it to keep blood off the seats on the way into town. Doc Olsen would be as relieved as I was to have a live customer to work on, this time.

TWENTY-FIVE

Peaceful bend was anything but peaceful over the next seven days.

Out-of-area and out-of-state visitors deluged the town and the sheriff's office, mostly in response to Lester's exclusive story but with the two local murders providing additional sensation and spice. A pair of Denver police officers with a legal warrant to take Harriet Greenley off our hands and back to Colorado. Newspapermen from Missoula, Kalispell, Helena (one bird from there referred to Peaceful Valley as "the new homicide capital of Montana"), Butte, and Billings, and from as far away as Denver, Cheyenne, and Spokane. Curiosity seekers from neighboring counties. Even a few drummers looking to capitalize on the publicity by selling people a lot of junk they didn't need.

All anybody wanted to talk about was the Greenley woman and/or Tyler Fix and the Axthelm family. She wouldn't speak to the reporters who came before she was hauled away, and neither would Bob Axthelm, sullen and suffering with his bullet-ripped cheek swathed in bandages, so they swarmed all over Carse and me. Mainly me. I had to answer so many questions and correct so much gossip-borne misinformation I developed a headache that plagued me for three days and spoiled my sleep three nights. The fact that just about everybody insisted on draping me in a hero's cloak didn't improve my disposition any. Neither did Clyde Senior suggesting the town hold a parade in my honor, a fool notion that I squelched in a hurry.

Far as I could tell, with all of this tumult going on there were only two people in the valley who still gave a fig about the disappearance and reappearance of the Cuba Libre wooden Indian, most having tucked it away as inconsequential if they hadn't already forgotten it entirely. Henry Bandelier was one who had it on his mind, of course. And I was the other. I could've just tucked it away myself, the devil with Bandelier, but I'm not made that way. It was the crime that had started the crime wave and the only one of the bunch that had yet to be brought to a satisfactory resolution.

What with one thing and another, it was Saturday a week before I saw my way clear to driving out to the reservation to see Tom Black Wolf and Charlie Walks Far. I went then because my headache had gone with the last of the clamoring visitors, the day was half-sunny and mild—a temporary break in the cold snap—and I knew I wouldn't have any peace of mind until the matter was cleared up. The history book I'd borrowed from Mary Ellen Belknap rode on the seat beside me in the flivver.

I found Tom at his house, bareheaded and in shirtsleeves, splitting jack pine chunks into cordwood. Charlie was helping him, loading the wood into Tom's wagon. They hadn't stopped working when they heard me coming, and didn't until I parked and walked around to where they were.

"Morning, boys," I said. "Kind of late in the season to be storing up wood for winter, seems like."

Tom dug his ax blade into the chopping block, brushed fingers through his sweat-damp hair. He didn't look at the book in my hand, but he could hardly have missed seeing it. His copper-toned face was impassive. "This wood is not for us," he said. "It is for an elder, Mrs. Running Bear."

Widow woman nearing eighty, as I recalled. "Good of you to make sure she's well provided for. Another long, cold winter coming up."

He had nothing to say to that. Neither did Charlie, standing a few feet away by the wagon. Waiting, both of them.

I said, "I was sorry to hear about your grandfather, Tom. Not unexpected, but a hard loss just the same."

A brief chin dip. Then, "Chief Victor was a great warrior in this world. He is now one in the next."

"I understand from Mr. Fetters the tribe honored him with ceremonial singing and dancing and a big feast. Burial according to custom afterwards, I expect."

"Yes."

"In the usual kind of box."

"Yes."

"But that wasn't the kind he wanted toward the end, was it? He craved a different sort of resting place for his mortal remains, one he took to be more befitting of his status as a great chief."

Tom said, slow, "He was very old. And very ill in his last days, in mind as well as body."

"He could read and write English, couldn't he?"

"Yes."

"Read some of the books you borrowed from Miss Belknap at the high school while he was lying abed, before the doctor moved him to the infirmary."

"He was not able to read then; I read to him. He only looked at the books."

"Uh-huh. This one here"—I held it up—"that you returned to Miss Belknap after he passed on. Got a torn and repaired page in it. But it wasn't you who damaged it, was it, Tom? It was Chief Victor."

"By accident. He wished to show the photograph to me, but his hands were not steady and the page tore."

"Interesting book. *Sons and Daughters of the Nile: A History of Egypt from Ancient to Modern Times.*" I opened it to the repaired page and held that up for emphasis.

Tom didn't look at it. His eyes were fixed unblinking on mine.

"Photograph of a sarcophagus," I said. "What the Egyptians buried their royalty in. That's what Chief Victor wanted or thought he wanted in his delirium—his own private Indian mummy case."

Charlie said, speaking for the first time, "Tom tried to argue with him. So did I. He would not listen."

"Uh-huh. And you, Tom, couldn't refuse to honor his last wish, daft and heretical as it was. Not while he was alive. You could've just pretended to do his bidding, but that would've been disloyal. Wasn't enough time to build a sarcophagus in his true likeness, so you hatched the idea of stealing Henry Bandelier's wooden Indian, sawing it in half, and chiseling out the insides."

Tom didn't say anything. Didn't need to. He knew what a dunderheaded idea it'd been without me telling him.

"But once you had the statue and cut into it," I said, "you realized it was a solid hunk of wood and that it'd take days, maybe weeks, to halve and hollow it and there wasn't enough time for that, either. I won't ask would you have gone ahead anyway if Chief Victor hadn't died when he did. Doesn't matter now. After the burial ceremony was over, you and Charlie did a careful repair job on the cut—"

"No. We did that before Chief Victor died, when we realized we could not honor his last wish."

"Must've been a real hard time for you. Point is, that night you went to wherever you had the statue hid, loaded it on your wagon, and took it back where you got it."

"It was only right that we do so."

"No argument there. But you know taking it in the first place was a crime, compounded by the saw-cut damage. Henry Bandelier has every legal right to press charges against you both. And he surely will, the minute he's notified that you've confessed."

Tom nodded, solemn. Charlie said, "Have you come to take us to jail, Sheriff Monk?"

"No need for that. I know you're not going to run off."

"What will you do?"

"Well, I can put a word in on your behalf with the county attorney, and I don't doubt he'd agree to let you stay free until the date of your trial. Don't doubt, either, that I could trust you to appear in court on the specified day and time."

Nods from both this time.

"Problem with that is," I said, "it might not be in your best interest. If I know Judge Peterson, he'd find you guilty on both counts and fine you each a minimum of fifty dollars and/or sentence you to thirty days on the county work farm. I don't suppose you could raise a hundred dollars between you?"

Tom said, "No."

Charlie said, "Not half that much."

"Either way, the felony convictions would be on your records, make jobs harder to come by. How much money you reckon you have between you? In your pockets right now, I mean."

"Very little," Tom said.

"Very little," Charlie said, like an echo.

"Have a look-see."

They rummaged through their pockets without question, Indians being used to obeying orders from white men in positions of authority. Tom had three rumpled dollar bills and a two-bit piece. Charlie had one dollar and nine cents, all in coins.

"Four dollars and thirty-two cents, total," I said. I held out my hand, palm up. "Let's have it, boys."

Again they obeyed, Charlie stoic, Tom with a puzzled side tilt of his head.

"This'll do. And if you're thinking the four bucks and change is a bribe, you're wrong. As sheriff, I'm entitled to set an alternate fine in any amount I choose, if in my discretion it's warranted, in order to save the county the expense of a trial. I don't have to notify Bandelier or Mr. Rademacher, or even file a report." All of which was hogwash, and Tom, at least, knew it. Seemed to me he came as close to smiling as an Indian ever does. "Your fines for the charges involving the theft and damage of that wooden Indian are a combined four dollars and thirty-two cents, payment of which amount closes the case permanent. Now we'll go inside and I'll write you out a receipt."

WHEN I GOT back to town, I took the $4.32 over to the Methodist church and put it in Reverend Noakes' feed-and-clothe-the-needy box.

Case resolved and closed.

Five cases resolved and closed, the crime wave now over and done with . . . I hoped.

TWENTY-SIX

THE HOPE TURNED out to be true. The crime wave was over, all right.

For a while I couldn't help worrying that it wasn't, that something else bad would happen all of a sudden. But nothing did. Things soon settled back to what we considered "normal," meaning the way they were before the sudden spate of trouble started.

Winter came, and 1915, and the spate of long, cold, white months that ended with the spring thaw in April, and a short, dry summer, and all too quick the leaves on the cottonwoods and willows turned gold and the days cool and frosty again. Plenty happened during that year, of course. The war in Europe kept escalating and there was talk that President Wilson would soon have the U.S. joining the fight on the side of the Allies, but in rural Montana folks as usual were more concerned with what was taking place here at home. The big state news came less than a month after the crime wave ended, when the legislature finally passed a law giving women equal voting rights. Armed troops once again occupied Butte in response to labor unrest in the copper mines. The WCTU and other prohibitionists were pushing hard for a state referendum to make it illegal to drink, serve, or manufacture alcoholic beverages, a prospect which worried and angered more than half the male populace.

Harriet Greenley was tried and convicted of first-degree murder in Kansas City, the authorities there having won the jurisdictional squabble, but judges and juries are hard put to give a woman the death penalty even when she deserves it. She got a long prison sentence instead, and word was that the Denver authorities would extradite her back to Colorado and try her again there as soon as she was released. Here in Peaceful Valley, Bob Axthelm was convicted of willful manslaughter with a recommendation of leniency, Judge Peterson surprising everybody by agreeing with the recommendation and handing down a reasonably short sentence in Deer Lodge prison.

Grover Fix sold the mercantile and his farm at bargain prices and moved away, I never did find out where. J. T. Axthelm and his wife stayed, but he put up a TRESPASSERS WILL BE SHOT sign to protect their privacy, and they did their trading elsewhere for I never saw either of them in Peaceful Bend again after the trial.

Lester Smithfield accepted a job as a crime reporter and

columnist on the *Denver Post*, thanks to his exclusive scoop and a boost from his friend Jordan Unger, and sold the *Sentinel* to a young eager beaver from Bismarck, North Dakota. Tom Black Wolf went up to the college in Saskatchewan to pursue his dream of being an agronomist. Henry Bandelier chained his wooden Indian to a wall bolt to keep anybody else from stealing it, not that anybody ever would again, thereby making the thing even more of a public eyesore. Doc Olsen concluded he'd had enough of slicing up dead bodies and resigned as coroner, the job going to a new doctor who had moved his practice down from Bigfork. Laura Peabody got herself married to a ladies apparel salesman from Missoula. Ellie Rademacher kept trying to convince Clyde Senior to run for the legislature and Clyde Junior to study law at the university, and not having much luck in either case. Monahan's Saloon caught fire late of a summer night, nobody knew just how, and burned to the ground, which made the Ladies Aid Society and the WCTU happy, if not the railroad workers, farmhands, and young sports like Jack Vanner.

As for me, it was a good year. I expected poor old Buster to give up the ghost, but he went right on keeping me company and passing gas no matter what I fed him. Reba Purvis decided I wasn't suitable husband material after all, terminated her campaign to make me hubby number three, and once more set her cap for Titus Bedford. Hadn't succeeded in trapping him yet, but he was showing signs of weakening. I was reelected sheriff by the widest margin ever, and without having to do much stumping for votes. The worst crime I had to contend with was another attempt by the halfwit

Hovey brothers to sell bootleg hooch to the Indians. A raid on their property by Carse and Boone and me led to the discovery and destruction of their hidden still—something else that made the WCTU happy—and a year for each of them on the county work farm. And best of all, Katherine wrote from Bozeman that she and Jim were expecting their first and I'd be a proud granddaddy along about next Easter.

Peaceful Bend, Peaceful Valley.

Places living up to their names again.